WHAT A WEEK TO MAKE A MOVE

ROSIE RUSHTON

PUFFIN BOOKS

PUFFIN BOOKS

Published by the Penguin Group
Penguin Books Ltd, 80 Strand, London WC2R 0RL, England
Penguin Putnam Inc., 375 Hudson Street, New York, New York 10014, USA
Penguin Books Australia Ltd, Ringwood, Victoria, Australia
Penguin Books Canada Ltd, 10 Alcorn Avenue, Toronto, Ontario, Canada M4V 3B2
Penguin Books India (P) Ltd, 11 Community Centre, Panchsheel Park,
New Delhi – 110 017, India
Penguin Books (NZ) Ltd, Cnr Rosedale and Airborne Roads, Albany, Auckland,
New Zealand
Penguin Books (South Africa) (Pty) Ltd, 24 Sturdee Avenue, Rosebank 2196,
South Africa

On the World Wide Web at: www.penguin.com

Penguin Books Ltd, Registered Offices: 80 Strand, London WC2R ORL, England

First published 2001
2
Copyright © Rosie Rushton, 2001
All rights reserved

The moral right of the author has been asserted

Set in 10pt /14pt Folio

Made and printed in England by Clays Ltd, St Ives plc

British Library Cataloguing in Publication Data
A CIP catalogue record for this book is available from the British Library

ISBN 0–141–31073–1

MONDAY

7.00 a.m.

3 Plough Cottages, Cattle Hill, West Green, Dunchester.
Suffering from sleep deprivation and poor parenting

'That does it!' Tansy Meadows threw back the duvet and stomped across her bedroom.

'I'm so happy, I'm so happy, I'm so hap-hap-hap-happy!' The sound of her mother's discordant singing wafted up the stairs – as it had done for the last half an hour.

'Mum!' Tansy wrenched open the bedroom door and stormed out on to the landing. 'Shut up!'

'My world is complete, my heart's at your feeeeet, my life is sub-LIME ...'

'Mum!' Tansy winced as her mother screeched out a top note. It was bad enough having to endure her mother's attempts at singing at the best of times; after only five hours' sleep, it was the pits.

'Oh darling, you're up!' Clarity Meadows, clutching a bundle of incense sticks in one hand and a box of matches in the other, paused halfway up the stairs and glanced at her watch in surprise.

1

'It's only seven o'clock, sweetheart – you could have had another fifteen minutes in bed!'

'What? With you doing your Celine Dion impressions all over the house? Fat chance!'

Her mum pulled a face.

'Sorry,' she said, climbing the last few stairs to the landing and giving Tansy a hug. 'I wasn't thinking.'

That's nothing new, thought Tansy. Much as she loved her mother, she had accepted long ago that Clarity acted first and thought later – often with fairly dire consequences for her nearest and dearest. Just lately, Tansy had thought that her mum had finally stopped drifting through life in a state of bewildered confusion, and started to act like a normal thirty-something. Sadly, as her appalling behaviour the night before had proved, it had been a false hope.

'Tansy, you look exhausted!' exclaimed her mother, pushing past her and opening the door to her own bedroom.

'Well, that's hardly surprising, is it?' retorted Tansy, following her in and flopping down on the unmade bed. 'Do you know what time you got home last night?'

Her mother shrugged.

'About midnight, I guess,' she ventured, thrusting some incense sticks into a wooden holder.

'No, Mum,' sighed Tansy. 'It was one-fifteen. I was worried sick.'

'One-fifteen? Was it really?' Her mother seemed amazed. 'I had no idea.'

She sighed dreamily.

'Anyway, darling, you had no need to worry,' she smiled. 'I was with Henry.'

'Exactly,' muttered Tansy under her breath. 'I rest my case.'

Henry was the latest of her mother's admirers and easily the most bizarre. Tansy had always assumed that it was her mother who held the world record for dottiness – until she met Henry.

'Oh, Tansy, I had such a wonderful time!' Clarity struck a match, lit the incense and grinned at her daughter. 'And I've got so much to tell you! You won't believe what happened!'

'It's perfectly clear what happened!' retorted Tansy, jumping to her feet. 'You drank far too much and came home totally smashed, and then spent another hour laughing and banging doors and making it impossible for me to sleep.'

'I was not drunk!' protested her mother, looking aghast at the very idea. 'I was just very, very happy.'

She smiled coyly at Tansy.

'Shall I tell you why?'

'If you must,' sighed Tansy, wrinkling her nose and edging away from the curls of patchouli-scented smoke rising from the dressing table.

Her mother sat down on the edge of the bed and cupped her chin in her hands.

'It was so wonderful,' she murmured. 'Henry took me down to the river and then ... guess what?'

'I suppose,' Tansy commented dryly, 'it's too much to hope that you pushed him in?'

'Oh, Tansy, don't be like that!' pleaded her mother.
'Henry's a lovely man – what could you possibly have against him?'

'You want a list?' Tansy demanded, fiddling with the perfume bottles on her mother's dressing table. 'For one thing, he's ancient.'

'Sixty is not ancient,' protested her mother. 'Besides, he's very young at heart.'

'If you mean he dresses like an ageing hippy and behaves like an emotionally challenged ten-year-old, I agree,' continued Tansy. 'And he's bald and –'

'And he makes me feel wonderful!' finished her mother. 'You do want me to be happy, don't you?'

Her mother looked at her in such an appealing way that Tansy couldn't help smiling and giving her a hug.

'Of course I do, Mum!' she sighed.

'Well, Henry makes me ecstatically happy,' her mother enthused. 'Last night we were walking by the river and he took my hand and leaned towards me and kissed ...'

The thought of her mother kissing anyone in a public place was more than Tansy could bear first thing in the morning.

'Mum, you shouldn't be behaving like that! What about Laurence?'

Her mother sighed and shook her head in exasperation.

'I've told you a dozen times, Tansy,' she exclaimed. 'It's all over between me and Laurence.'

'But ...'

'Laurence was a dear in many ways,' her mother went on. 'We had some happy times, but he was ... well, you won't agree but ...'

'But what?'

'He was boring,' her mother declared emphatically.

There wasn't much Tansy could say. Her mother was right. Laurence could have bored for England. He worked for the Schools Library Service, had the haircut from hell, and thought he was a world expert on everything. There had been a time when her mum had considered moving in with him; luckily she had come to her senses when he had forbidden to let her burn incense or hang wind chimes in his house.

'No,' murmured her mother now. 'Laurence is just a dear friend. Whereas Henry ...'

The sentence hung unfinished in the air.

'... is dotty,' muttered Tansy. At least Laurence had never had sufficient imagination to lead her mother astray – he would never have kept her out until one in the morning. What's more he had his uses: he had taken Tansy and her mother skiing at New Year and, if Tansy had to put up with her mother behaving in a totally irresponsible manner, she would far rather have her doing it in a smart Swiss ski resort than hanging around Dunchester with a geriatric hippy.

'Henry,' her mother continued, interrupting her thoughts, 'is so much more romantic. And funny. And just adorable.'

'And nuts,' muttered Tansy, edging towards the door.

'What's the matter with you?' her mother demanded. 'Do you have to spoil everything?'

To Tansy's alarm, her mother's eyes had filled with tears.

'It's almost as if you don't want me to have a life,' Clarity went on. 'I'm not just a mother, you know. I'm a woman too. A woman with needs.'

Tansy opened her mouth to reply but her mother was in full flood.

'And what's more, I'm not getting any younger,' she continued. 'Life is passing me by.'

So that was it, thought Tansy. She should have guessed. It happened every year about this time. The closer her mother got to another birthday, the more manic she became and the more ridiculously she behaved. She would only be thirty-three on Saturday, which was heaps younger than the parents of Tansy's friends – but that didn't stop her being terrified of growing old.

'I want some fun,' her mother sighed plaintively. 'Before it's too late.'

Suddenly, Tansy felt rather guilty. After all, her mum had only been seventeen years old when Tansy was born. Tansy's father had disappeared without trace and her mum had been on her own ever since. She worked flat out as a landscape gardener in order to make ends meet; her life was hardly the stuff dreams were made of, and certainly not the kind of existence that Tansy was planning for herself.

'I'm sorry, Mum!' she said, running over to the bed and giving her mother a hug. 'If you really like Henry, that's fine by me.'

'Really? Do you mean that, darling?' Her mother looked up at her beseechingly.

'Sure I do,' nodded Tansy. 'It's your life, after all.'

And it's not as if it's going to affect me that much, I suppose, she thought.

'I'm so pleased you said that!' breathed her mother, giving Tansy's hand a squeeze. 'Because … well, do you know what Henry said to me last night?'

'No,' sighed Tansy, edging over to the door once again. 'But I've no doubt you are about to tell me.'

'He said,' her mother went on, 'that I was a ray of sunlight sent to lighten up the darkest corners of his life.'

'Oh vomit, yuk!' squirmed Tansy. 'That is so not cool!'

'And then he said something even more wonderful,' her mother enthused.

'That wouldn't be difficult,' murmured Tansy.

'He said that he wanted –'

'Later, Mum, OK?' interrupted Tansy, who had heard quite enough already. It was one thing to be understanding towards a parent, and quite another to indulge them by listening to the gory details of their love life. 'I'm going to have a shower.'

'But darling, you don't understand!' protested her mother. 'Henry–'

'Mum,' remarked Tansy as patiently as she could, 'if I waited to have a shower until I understood everything you say, I'd never get clean! Tell me later, OK?'

She didn't wait for her mother to reply, but shut the bathroom door firmly behind her and turned on the shower full blast. There were times when you simply had to be firm with parents.

7.30 a.m.

6 Kestrel Close, West Green, Dunchester.
Suffering from separation anxiety

'Won't you ever learn? How many more times do I have to tell you? You simply cannot go on spending money like this!'

Cleo Greenway hovered at the foot of the stairs and winced as the sound of her stepfather's voice reverberated from behind the closed kitchen door.

'But, darling, it was a snip, it really was – and, besides, I do so love to look pretty for you!'

Cleo sighed. Her mother had been shopping at the

weekend and clearly Roy was not impressed with the results. She could imagine her mother sidling up to Roy, putting her arms around his neck and gazing pleadingly into his eyes.

'You don't have the first idea, do you?' her stepfather exploded. 'You seem to think that I have a bottomless pit of money. Well, I don't!'

Cleo sighed and glanced at her watch. She hated it when her parents argued, but this morning they were actually doing her a favour. With a bit of luck they would be too busy winding one another up to notice what she was doing.

'Please God, let it be there!' she prayed, tiptoeing into the study and carefully closing the door behind her. Using the computer without asking was another thing that Roy went ballistic about. Most of her mates had PCs of their own, but her stepfather said that they were antisocial and bad for your eyes, and besides, one computer was enough for any family.

She switched on and dialled up Outlook Express.

'Come on, come on!' She tapped her fingers impatiently on the desk as the machine ground its way through the connection process.

'Things around here are going to have to change big time!' Roy's voice grew louder as the kitchen door was flung open. 'We simply can't go on like this!'

'Hurry!' Cleo ordered the computer.

Obligingly, the computer made its Internet connection. Cleo clicked the Inbox button.

'NO MESSAGES.'

'But there has to be!' she hissed at the screen, clicking the mouse again.

'NO MESSAGES.'

She felt sick. It had been three days. Three whole days without a word from Trig. No letter, no e-mail, no phone call. Not even a text message. He always sent text messages, even when he couldn't get through on the phone.

She couldn't bear it. What if he was ill? What if he had had an accident? She had tried phoning eight times over the weekend, and there had been no reply. Maybe the whole family were gathered by his hospital bedside.

Or maybe, she thought with a sinking feeling, he had met someone else at this new school of his and had been out with her all day every day. She knew from the movies that American High School kids were really sassy and clued up. What's more they were over there and she was stuck here, three thousand miles from the guy she loved.

'Oh terrific!' Her stepfather's irritable tones broke in on her thoughts. 'The mail has arrived! More bills, no doubt!'

She heard Roy striding down the hall to the front door, and jumped to her feet as the letterbox clattered and mail thudded to the floor. Her heart began pounding. Please God, let there be a letter. If you let there be a letter, I'll go to church every Sunday for the rest of eternity.

She switched off the computer and waited until Roy had thundered back into the kitchen. Then she slipped out of the study and followed him.

'Morning, darling!' Her mother was standing at the Aga, stirring a saucepan and looking rather flushed.

'Scrambled eggs?'

Cleo shook her head.

'I'm not hungry,' she mumbled.

'Not hungry?' Diana Greenway looked astounded. 'Darling, you are always hungry.'

'Well, I'm not now, OK?' Cleo snapped, scanning the wad of letters in her stepfather's hand in the hope of seeing an airmail envelope.

'Anything for me?' she asked, trying to sound casual as she flopped down at the kitchen table.

'Give me a chance,' muttered Roy, flipping through the letters.

'Looking for a letter from lover boy, are we?' teased Portia, her seventeen-year-old sister, who was nibbling a piece of toast.

'I wish I had a boyfriend,' sighed Lettie, her younger sister.

'Don't be silly, sweetheart – you're only eleven!' laughed her mother. 'Plenty of time for all that.'

'They're not worth it, Lettie,' drawled Portia, pushing back her chair and standing up. 'They make you pale, miserable and spotty – look at Cleo!'

'Oh go boil your head!' spat Cleo.

Portia grinned, grabbed her leather jacket from the back of the chair and gave her mother a peck on the cheek.

'I'm off,' she said.

'Good,' said Cleo. 'Don't hurry back.'

Portia stuck out her tongue and flounced merrily out of the door.

'Bills, bills, bills – that's all we ever get!' Roy complained, tossing the letters one by one on to the kitchen table. 'Who's this for?'

He peered at a bright-pink envelope.

Cleo held her breath.

'Lettie,' he said.

'Goodie!' cried Lettie, jumping up from the table and ripping open the envelope. 'Party invitation.'

'Oh, and that one's for you!'

He flung a brown envelope across the room at Diana.

'That's the lot,' he sighed, tossing a circular about double glazing into the pedal bin.

Cleo's heart sank. She felt like bursting into tears. Nothing from Trig. She didn't think she could bear it.

When Trig's father had been offered a high-powered job back home in Illinois, Trig had promised faithfully that he would be in touch with her every day. And to begin with, he had kept his word. OK, so she had always phoned him a lot more than he had phoned her – but that was because the time difference made things difficult and, besides, she could never manage to wait until the pre-arranged time for his call to come through. Whenever she had a spare minute to herself, she would call him and they would talk for ages. And when phoning was impossible, she sent him e-mails and text messages as well as letters that were pages long.

Only, just lately, the replies had been getting further and further apart and the phone calls shorter and shorter. Trig always seemed to be dashing off somewhere. And then, three days ago, the letters and messages had stopped altogether.

Surely, if he loved her as much as she loved him, he couldn't survive without calling her. Something terrible must have happened to him. She just knew it.

'Darling, you must eat – I insist!' Her mother put a plate of toast in front of her. Cleo pushed it away. The sight of the melting butter made her feel sick.

She glanced at the clock. She couldn't phone him now – it was the middle of the night in America and his parents would go ballistic if she woke them.

But, she thought suddenly, what if she rang him on

his mobile? He always had it with him – he was addicted to the games. It was bound to be in his bedroom and she could talk to him without his parents knowing.

That's what she would do! She would call him on the way to school on her mobile phone. She knew it would cost a fortune, but she'd worry about that later. And Trig wouldn't mind being woken up – not for love.

When you were in love, sleep didn't matter.

7.40 a.m.

Wishing and hoping – and sighing a lot

Holly Vine stared across the damp lawn and into the uncurtained window of the house at the end of the garden. Paul's house. She sighed deeply. Why, out of all the guys in Dunchester, did she have to fall for the only one who wasn't remotely interested in girls? When Paul had told her that he wanted the two of them to be 'just friends', which had to be the most doom-laden phrase ever invented, she had tried desperately to stop thinking about him, to give up gazing at his house every morning just in the hope of seeing him.

It hadn't worked. Four months on, she still adored him. When they bumped into one another – which wasn't often enough, because he went to Bishop Agnew College on the far side of town – her heart still pounded in her chest and she felt as if her knees would give way underneath her.

But, she told herself firmly, turning away from the window and picking up her hairbrush, it had to stop. She would have to find someone else, forget about Paul and get on with her life. After all, she was in Year Ten now and to be single in Year Ten was simply not on. Tansy had Andy Richards, Jade had Scott, and Cleo had Trig – even though he was half a world away.

The only person in the whole year who didn't have a guy in tow was Allegra Webb, Jade's cousin. And she was doing her utmost to seduce every guy in sight.

I have to get a boy before Allegra, Holly told herself firmly.

The trouble was, anyone but Paul would be second best. She would be in love with Paul till the day she died. And she'd probably die very young from a broken heart.

Her life was tragic.

Shakespeare would have had a ball.

7.45 a.m.

53 Lime Avenue, Oak Hill, Dunchester. Trying to escape

'Jade, wait for me!'

Jade Williams paused in the hall and sighed as the sound of her cousin's pleading voice wafted down the stairs.

'I can't, Allegra!' she called back. 'I've got to get to school early to ...' She racked her brains to think up a believable excuse. '... sort something out,' she ended feebly.

Well, it wasn't so much of a lie, she comforted herself, shrugging her arms into the sleeves of her jacket and picking up her school bag.

She did have something to sort out.

Her entire life.

She had someone to sort out too.

Scott.

Besides, she just wanted to have a few minutes all to herself without Allegra quizzing her on the personal history of every guy at West Green Upper School. And without Scott. Definitely without Scott.

She glanced at her watch. If she didn't get going right now, Scott would be on the doorstep, wanting to walk with her. And she knew exactly what he would say.

'Are you going off me?'

'Why didn't you come over on Saturday?'

'I love you, Jade. I want to be with you all the time!'

Three months ago, that would have sent a thrill of excitement through her; now it just made her feel irritated.

'I'm coming, honestly! Just two more minutes!' Allegra called down the stairs.

Jade knew what Allegra's idea of two minutes was like. By the time she had curled her eyelashes, and applied her lip gloss and tried her hair in a dozen different styles, it would be eight o'clock and Scott would be ringing the doorbell.

Jade grabbed her bag.

'Sorry, must dash!'

She slammed the front door behind her and sped down the path. She turned left and didn't stop running until she had rounded the corner and was out of sight of the house.

It was odd, she thought. A year ago, when she had first moved in with her aunt's family after the death of both her parents in a car crash, Allegra had done all she could to make her life a misery. She had resented having to share her bedroom with Jade, told her that she was pathetic and babyish, and generally been a little sneak whenever the opportunity arose. A year ago, Jade would have given anything for Allegra to want her company.

Now, though, things were different; Allegra had left her stage school and had been in Year Ten – the same year as Jade – at West Green Upper School for half a term. Jade wished she had been put in Year Eleven like everyone else her age, but she was so behind with coursework that the Head had insisted on her repeating a year.

And, suddenly, Jade was flavour of the month; Allegra was always hanging round her, and Jade was getting sick of it. It was a pity, she thought, that Allegra didn't fancy Scott Hamill.

If she did, that would be both problems solved.

7.50 a.m.

6 Kestrel Close. About to face the music

'I'm off!' Cleo grabbed her school bag and gave her mother a peck on the cheek. 'I'll be back at ...'

'Wait! Oh look – oh joy!' Her mother had ripped open her envelope and was waving a sheaf of papers in the air. 'I've got an audition!'

Diana Greenway had been a Shakespearean actress years before and, despite having spent more time out of work than in it recently, she had never lost the ability to be dramatic at the drop of a hat.

'What for?' Cleo asked suspiciously, her hand hovering over the door knob. Ever since her mother had appeared on national television clad in nothing but her bra and knickers,

Cleo had prayed that she would give up all ideas of stardom and get a normal job like other mothers.

'It's a TV play, darling!' her mother exclaimed excitedly, running her eyes over the script. 'It looks like a marvellous part – I'm to play a middle-aged woman who is slowly going mad.'

'Do you think you'll get it?' Roy asked hopefully, looking up from his mail.

'Bound to,' muttered Cleo. 'She won't have to act at all – it's perfect type-casting.'

'Oh, darling, really! You are too naughty!' laughed Diana as Cleo opened the door. 'But, wait, you're not going, surely? You haven't eaten.'

Cleo grabbed a banana from the fruit bowl.

'I'll eat this on the way,' she said.

'Not enough,' declared Diana firmly. 'Eat that toast before you –'

'For God's sake, what is this?'

Cleo's stepfather suddenly leapt to his feet and stabbed at a sheet of paper with his finger.

'It's a phone bill,' murmured Cleo's mother vaguely.

'Oh, how observant!' retorted Roy sarcastically. 'And perhaps you would care to cast an eye over the figure at the bottom of the page.'

'Two hundred and eighty-five pounds,' read Diana. 'Isn't that rather a lot?'

'Isn't that rather a lot?' mimicked Roy. 'Yes it is – it's at least seventy-five pounds more than usual. And I suppose I have you to blame?'

He glared at his wife.

'Me?' Diana looked injured. 'Why me?'

'It's all down here!' he shouted, slapping the itemized

sheets with his hand. 'I don't imagine anyone else is telephoning the United States for hours on end!'

Cleo's stomach did a rather impressive double somersault and she edged towards the door.

'What is it, Diana?' bellowed Roy. 'Dreams of a starring rôle in Hollywood, is it? Chatting up some slimy film director in LA, is that it?'

Cleo paused. She couldn't let her mother take the blame. But then again ...

'No it is not!' cried Diana. 'I haven't telephoned America in months. I don't even know anyone over there any more – well, apart from Cleo's little friend, of course ... oh!'

Her voice faltered as her eyes met Cleo's.

'She's been phoning Trig loads of times,' interrupted Lettie smugly. 'I've heard her – all slushy, gooey, kissy-kissy stuff! Yuk!'

Cleo lunged at her but Lettie simply stuck out her tongue and ran out of the room. God, I wish I was an only child, thought Cleo.

'Cleopatra!' Her stepfather's face had turned purple and he appeared to be struggling to breathe. 'Have you been making calls to America without permission?'

Cleo looked at the floor.

'Occasionally,' she muttered.

'Occasionally!' spluttered Roy. 'Look at that!'

He snatched the bill from Diana's hand.

'Fifth of September – four pounds seventy, Fifth of September – same day, see? – Nine pounds fifteen! Nine pounds fifteen!'

He gripped the back of the chair.

'And there's more – four pounds on the seventh of

September, five pounds twenty on the eighth, five pounds thirty-five on the tenth … weeks and weeks of it!'

'Sorry!' said Cleo, largely because she couldn't think of anything else to say.

'Sorry? Oh you will be, believe me!' stormed Roy. 'I'm going to call that telephone company right now and get them to put a bar on all international calls!'

'You can't!' cried Cleo. 'Trig's my boyfriend! I miss him!' She felt her eyes filling with tears.

'So write letters!' retorted her stepfather. 'Call him from a pay phone with your own money. Just don't expect me to fund your adolescent crushes!'

He strode towards the phone.

'Mum!' Cleo cried. 'Do something.'

Her mother nibbled a fingernail.

'You pop off to school, darling,' she whispered. 'I'll calm him down. I'll sort it.'

She squeezed Cleo's hand.

'Promise?' begged Cleo.

'I promise,' her mum assured her. 'Don't you worry.'

8 a.m.

3 Plough Cottages, Cattle Hill, West Green, Dunchester
In for a shock – big time

'Now darling,' began Tansy's mother as Tansy flopped into a chair and poured muesli into a bowl. 'I must talk to you about Henry …'

'What about Henry?' muttered Tansy.

'He's coming round later and I thought I should –'

'Again!' spluttered Tansy, spitting cereal all over the

breakfast table. 'You only saw him last night.'

She eyed her mother anxiously.

'You know, Mum, you should never let a guy think he can hang around whenever the mood takes him ...'

'Oh darling!' giggled her mother. 'You are funny. And, anyway, Henry is going to be hanging around, as you call it, a great deal in the future.' She took a deep breath.

'You see, we're getting married.'

Tansy felt as if all the blood in her veins had turned to ice. She stared at her mother.

'Married?'

Her mother nodded.

'Henry asked me last night.' She took another deep breath. 'And I said yes.'

'But you can't!' Tansy exploded, pushing her breakfast to one side and leaping to her feet. 'I mean, it's obscene! He's old enough to be your father!'

'I love him, darling!' Clarity replied beseechingly. 'Age doesn't matter when you meet the right person.'

'But he's not the right person!' Tansy shouted, a sob catching in her throat. 'For God's sake, Mum, you've only known the guy a couple of months.'

'Fourteen weeks and three days, actually,' sighed her mother. 'The best three months of my life.'

She put an arm around Tansy's shoulder.

'Darling, I didn't want you to find out like this,' she began. 'I wanted to sit down and talk it through and make you see how wonderful life is going to be ...'

'Wonderful!' Tansy looked at her as if she had suddenly lost her mind. 'It will be awful.'

'Just think, sweetheart, we'll have someone to look after us and –'

'But, Mum,' pleaded Tansy, 'we've managed all right up to now, haven't we? We've got one another – we don't need anyone else.'

'I do,' insisted her mother. 'I want to be loved and cherished and made a fuss of.'

'So go out with the guy – go out with a hundred different guys for all I care, but please, Mum, don't get married!' Tansy implored her, her heart pounding and her eyes filling with angry tears.

Her mother put her elbows on the table and rested her head in her hands.

'Look, darling, let's talk about this later, when you're calmer,' she suggested. 'You've got to get off to school and you'll see, once you get used to the idea –'

'I'll never get used to the idea!' shouted Tansy. 'It stinks!'

She jumped up, pushed her mother out of the way and grabbed her jacket from the hook by the back door.

'Anyway, he's been married before! He's got grown-up kids, for heaven's sake! You told me! So that proves he's unreliable, doesn't it?'

To Tansy's annoyance, her mother just laughed.

'Darling, that was twenty years ago. And his wife was an absolute witch – he told me. Poor love, he's been on his own ever since.'

'Probably because no one else would be daft enough to have him!' snapped Tansy.

'Tansy, don't be like this!' pleaded her mother. 'This is my life, and for once, I have to do what's right for me!'

'Fine!' Tansy pulled open the back door. 'Do it! Wreck your life if you must, but don't expect me to join in the celebrations!'

She slammed the door, squeezed past her mother's

battered pick-up truck and unbolted the back gate.

And ran slap bang into Henry Fazackerley's vast stomach.

'Morning, kiddo! Gimme five!'

He held up his hand to slap hers. Once, his sheer stupidity would have made her laugh, but this morning she simply felt sick. She turned away in disgust.

'And how are you this beautiful morning?' Henry blustered on.

She wanted to say something cutting. Or witty. Or just plain rude.

She opened her mouth but nothing came out.

Instead, she looked at him standing there, his stomach sticking over the top of his faded denim jeans, and his long grey hair tied back in a ponytail, and she wanted to cry.

'Has your mum told you the wonderful news?' Henry boomed, tickling her under the chin as though she was four years old.

That did it.

'Wonderful news? No!' glowered Tansy. 'She hasn't told me anything remotely wonderful all morning.'

'Well, hang on for a moment and –'

He was interrupted by a quick burst of 'When the Saints Go Marching In' emanating from his back pocket.

'Sorry – phone!'

He pulled out a purple phone.

'Who? Sorry, can I call you back? I'm in the middle of something really big.'

He winked at Tansy and snapped his phone cover shut.

'Have I got a surprise for you!' he said, slapping Tansy on the back.

'I think,' she spat back, as her mother opened the back door, 'that I've had quite enough surprises for one morning!'

And with that she pushed past him and ran down the hill.

'Tansy – wait!' Her mother's voice wafted through the gate after her, but she just kept running. She had no intention of waiting.

She had some very serious thinking to do. Her mother might think she was going to marry Henry Fazackerley, but Tansy was equally determined that she wasn't.

It was, after all, a daughter's duty to protect a parent from their own stupidity.

8.25 a.m.

On the way to school. Miffed

'You stupid, stupid phone!'

Cleo hurled her mobile phone back into her school bag and struggled not to cry.

It was all her stepfather's fault. All her mates had phone accounts – but Roy had insisted that she had to have a Pay As You Go phone. Now her top-up card had run out, and she hadn't got enough money on her to get another – and that meant she couldn't phone Trig.

But she had to phone him. She couldn't get through another day without hearing the sound of his voice. She had to find a way, whatever it took.

8.35 a.m.

On the way to school. Numb inside

She couldn't marry him, Tansy thought, kicking a stray drinks can into the gutter. She wouldn't marry him. It would be OK — she was probably tipsy the night before and said yes without thinking. Once she saw him again, in the cold light of day, she would realize that marriage was out of the question.

She would. Wouldn't she?

8.40 a.m.

In the schoolyard

'Have you seen Jade?' Scott Hamill tapped Holly on the shoulder as she headed towards the main entrance.

'Nope.'

Scott sighed.

'I called at her house and her aunt said she'd already left,' he sighed.

Holly looked at him pityingly.

'So,' she said with exaggerated patience, 'you'll see her some time today, right?'

Scott nodded.

'Yes, b-but ... Holly?' he stammered.

'What?'

'Has Jade said anything to you about me?' he asked.

'You mean, other than mentioning your name every five minutes,' Holly teased.

'She does?' Scott brightened visibly.

'Sure,' nodded Holly. 'Obsessed, she is.'

'Cool,' said Scott, looking smug. 'Tell her I was looking for her, OK?'

'OK,' sighed Holly.

8.50 a.m.

In the locker room. West Green Upper School

'Hi, Jade!' Holly pushed her way through the crush and tapped Jade on the shoulder. 'Scott's looking for you. He's in a right tizz.'

Jade glanced over her shoulder at Holly and raised her eyebrows.

'Surprise, surprise!' she sighed. 'I just wish he'd leave me alone – it's like being followed around by a small puppy!'

Holly's eyes widened. Jade and Scott were an item – everyone knew how much she adored him and how devastated she had been when they had had a major bust-up a few months earlier.

'Have you two had a row?' she asked, dumping her schoolbag on the floor and fishing in her pocket for her lip gloss.

'Not yet,' muttered Jade. 'But if he goes on like this we soon will do!'

'Like what?' asked Holly through puckered lips.

'Ringing me five times a day, asking whether I still love him, expecting me to spend the whole weekend with him ...'

'What's wrong with any of that?' demanded Holly. 'You should be so lucky.'

'You'd get sick of it if Paul carried on that way,' Jade reasoned.

'No, I wouldn't!' retorted Holly. 'Not that there's any chance of it ever happening. Paul just wants us to be friends.' She sighed. 'The thing is, I'm not suited to platonic relationships. I'm a very passionate person.'

'Perhaps you should use your powers of seduction on Scott,' teased Jade. 'Get him off my back.'

'You don't mean that,' Holly laughed, nudging Jade's arm.

'I don't know what I mean,' sighed Jade. 'I mean, I'm really fond of Scott and I don't want to hurt his feelings, but I can't bear the way he suffocates me. I don't know what to do.'

'Well, you'd better make your mind up,' urged Holly. 'Because he's heading this way.' She jerked her head in the direction of the door. 'Hey – where are you going?'

'Anywhere Scott isn't!' hissed Jade, grabbing her backpack and setting off in the opposite direction. 'At least we're in different classes this year.'

She dodged behind a pillar.

'And you haven't seen me, OK?'

Some people, thought Holly, don't know when they're well off.

8.55 a.m.

Heading for Registration

'Hi, Cleo!' Holly bounded up the stairs two at a time and grabbed Cleo's arm as she turned into the corridor. 'You'll never guess what! Jade says that Scott ... hey, what's the matter?'

'Nothing!'

'Oh, sure!' protested Holly. 'You've been crying.'

'So?'

'So can I help?'

'No,' sighed Cleo. 'That is ... well ...'

'What?'

Cleo paused outside the classroom.

'You couldn't possibly lend me some money, could you? I'll pay you back tomorrow.'

'Sure' shrugged Holly. 'How much do you want?'

Cleo swallowed.

'Ten pounds,' she blurted out.

'TEN POUNDS?'

Holly stared at her.

'I need to buy a top-up phone card, and they don't come any cheaper than ten pounds,' gabbled Cleo. 'It's really urgent. I have to phone Trig ...'

'Oh, Cleo – you're not still pining after Trig, are you?' sighed Holly. 'I mean, it's been three months since he left and –'

'What's that got to do with it?' Cleo demanded, pushing open the classroom door. 'You don't just stop loving someone because they've gone away.'

'I know, I'm sorry,' Holly said placatingly. 'I can lend you one pound fifty.'

'Thanks!' Cleo practically snatched the coins from Holly's hand and stuffed them in her skirt pocket.

'But,' advised Holly, 'it would be much cheaper to phone from home.'

'Oh shut up!' Cleo snapped. 'What do you know about anything?'

Not enough, sighed Holly to herself as Cleo flounced through the swing doors into the classroom. And if I don't find a real man soon, my reputation will be in shreds.

Two minutes later

'Where were you? I waited for ages!' Scott blocked Jade's way as she headed for the door.

'What? Oh – I had to deliver a letter for Auntie Paula,' she said hurriedly. 'Sorry.'

Why can't I just tell him straight? Why do I have to lie?

'You might have said,' complained Scott. 'I was worried. I missed you.'

'Oh for heaven's sake!' Jade blurted out. 'I'm here now, aren't I? Anyway, I have got to dash or I'll be late for French.'

'See you at breaktime?' Scott asked.

'I suppose,' murmured Jade.

'What?'

'I said yes, of course, I'll see you at break,' she smiled. And wished she could feel excited about it.

8.58 a.m.

Outside the classroom

'Hey, Tansy! Wait!' Andy, her boyfriend, pounded up the stairs after her. 'You will never believe what my mother has gone and done now.'

Tansy gave a short laugh.

'Believe me, it will be nothing compared with what mine has done.'

Andy sighed.

'Mum's only turning me out of my bedroom to make room for these wretched babies when they arrive,' he said. 'She expects me to share with Ricky – and that is so not on!'

'You call that a problem?' replied Tansy. 'My mum's decided to get married.'

'Married?' Andy gasped. 'But that's cool!'

'WHAT?' Tansy stared at him pityingly.

'Well, Laurence isn't such a bad guy and –'

'She's not marrying Laurence,' retorted Tansy. 'She's marrying Henry.'

'Henry?' Andy looked puzzled. 'Who on earth is Henry?'

'Exactly,' sighed Tansy.

9 a.m.

In registration

'Holly Vine?'

'Here, sir.'

'Allegra Webb?'

'Here, sir.'

'Tom ...' Mr Grubb's head jerked up from the register as the double doors crashed together and Tansy Meadows burst into the classroom.

'Sorry I'm late, sir!' she mumbled.

'And why are you late, Miss Meadows?' demanded Mr Grubb, tapping his pencil impatiently on the table. 'Overslept, did you?'

'No, sir,' she mumbled.

'Forgot our homework and had to go back for it, did we?'

Clearly Mr Grubb was having a bad day.

'Family crisis, sir,' she retorted. 'And I'd rather not talk about it in public.'

'Hrrrrm' grunted Mr Grubb, which was teacher-speak

for 'Oh bother, now I have to be nice to her.'

'What crisis?' muttered Holly as Tansy slumped down in the chair beside her, catching her breath.

'Later,' hissed Tansy. 'If I talk about it now, I'll throw up.'

9.05 a.m.

On the way to French

'Married?' Holly stared at her best friend in astonishment. 'Your mum?'

Tansy nodded miserably.

'So Laurence finally popped the question ...?'

'Not Laurence, Henry.'

'Henry?' Holly's eyes widened in disbelief. 'The bald one? The one with the bandana and the earring – the guy she took to the pop concert?'

Tansy nodded again.

'Oh,' said Holly. 'Right.'

'Is that all you can say?' demanded Tansy.

'I'm trying,' said Holly, 'to be polite.'

'Don't bother,' replied Tansy. 'Say what you think.'

'Yuk, yuk, and double yuk,' said Holly.

9.10 a.m.

In French

'Is it true –' Jade nudged Tansy's arm while Mrs Chapman was scribbling on the board – 'that your mum's getting married to that Henry guy?'

'Not if I can help it,' muttered Tansy and turned away because to her horror, her eyes had filled with tears.

'Don't worry,' said Jade comfortingly. 'It might never happen. They might have an almighty bust-up, you never know.'

'I live in hope,' sighed Tansy.

9.30 a.m.

Still in French

> Dear Holly,
> What does 'dis-lui bien des choses de ma part' mean? I make it 'ten somethings well the things of my part' but that doesn't make sense. Please tell me - Mrs C. says if I get another C-minus, she'll put me on French detention. I asked Tansy but she keeps ignoring me. Love, Cleo

> Dear Cleo,
> You're nuts! It means 'Give him my love.' Mind you, why the French have to use so many words beats me. Anyway, talking of love - did you know that Tansy's mum is going to marry Henry? The guy she took to the pop concert when Allegra got drunk, remember?
> Tansy's really cut up about it. That's why she's sitting there in a trance.

'That is SO romantic!' whispered Cleo, scrunching up the note and stuffing it in her pocket.

'I suggest,' murmured Holly, 'that you don't share that opinion with Tansy.'

'Why not?'

'Because she just might wring your neck.'

10.45 a.m.

Break time. In the school yard. Pacing about a lot

'I've got to stop her!' declared Tansy for the fifth time. 'It's madness.'

'Like I said, it might not happen,' Jade reassured her. 'Weddings take ages to organize and they could easily go off one another.'

'Is he rich?' asked Holly.

'Dunno,' Tansy shrugged. 'Does it matter?'

'It helps,' grinned Holly.

'That is so not true!' Cleo burst out. 'Love is all that matters – I'd rather be destitute with the guy I loved than living in a mansion with the wrong man.'

'Mmm,' murmured Holly. 'I guess.'

'You could get your mum to meet a whole load of other men,' suggested Jade. 'You know, really dishy types ...'

'Oh sure!' exclaimed Tansy. 'And just where in Dunchester am I likely to find them?'

'True,' sighed Jade.

'I know!' cried Holly. 'Pine.'

'I beg your pardon?' asked Tansy.

'Start mooning around, go all pale, cry a lot, stop eating ...'

'Stop eating?' Tansy looked incredulous.

'Tansy,' said Holly sternly. 'Drastic situations call for drastic remedies.'

'I suppose,' sighed Tansy. 'You don't suppose kids are allowed to take out court orders to restrain irresponsible parents, do you?'

Holly shook her head.

'She's over eighteen – she can do what she likes.'

'That,' sighed Tansy, 'is what worries me.'

Five minutes later

'I've been looking everywhere for you!' Scott Hamill grabbed Jade's arm. 'Where were you?'

'I was … er, helping Holly and Tansy sort something out,' she said. 'Sorry.'

'So, will you come round tonight?' Scott asked eagerly. 'We could do our homework together and then play my new computer game – it's really good! There's this –'

'Sorry, Scott, but I can't tonight,' Jade interrupted hastily. 'I'm going out.'

'Out? Where? Who with?'

'Oh – family outing. Pizza and bowling. A treat for Helen,' she improvised hastily, thinking that even Scott wouldn't want to muscle in on an eight-year-old's evening out.

Scott sighed.

'So tomorrow? Promise you'll come round tomorrow?'

'Sure I will,' agreed Jade, trying to sound enthusiastic.

'I love you,' Scott whispered, brushing Jade's neck with his lips.

'Mmm, me too,' she replied, squeezing his hand.

She was pretty sure that it wasn't true any more, but she knew it was what he wanted to hear and she couldn't bear to hurt his feelings. Maybe if she really tried, the old feelings would come back.

And then everyone would be happy.

1.05 p.m.

£££

In the school cafeteria

'Cleo,' observed Holly as she sat down to tackle what the school caterers had the audacity to call vegetable cannelloni, 'you're not eating.'

'I'm not hungry,' replied Cleo.

'You're always hungry,' remarked Tansy. 'Always.'

'Oh don't you start!' Cleo retorted, pushing her half-drunk can of cola to one side.

'Is something wrong?' asked Jade, peeling the wrapper off her packet of sandwiches.

'No! Yes!'

'She's pining,' observed Holly. 'For Trig.'

'What? Still?' Tansy frowned.

'Yes, still!' shouted Cleo. 'Just because you lot don't have deep relationships, you can't imagine what it's like to be really in love. Well, Trig and I have and we are and ...'

And then suddenly she was crying.

'Hey – I didn't mean to upset you!' Tansy cried, reaching out her hand. 'Can we help?'

'Could you lend me some money?'

'Here we go again,' muttered Holly under her breath.

'How much?' asked Tansy.

'Eight pounds fifty,' replied Cleo. 'I have to buy a phone card.'

Tansy hesitated.

'Well, I suppose I could lend you a tenner,' she said. 'Only you absolutely have to give it back to me tomorrow. I've got to buy my mum's birthday present.'

'I will, honestly, I promise!' Cleo brightened visibly. 'Thanks so much, Tansy. You don't know what that means.'

Tansy pulled out her purse and handed Cleo the ten-pound note.

'So now I can have my one pound fifty back?' queried Holly.

'Later!' cried Cleo, pushing back her chair and leaping to her feet. 'Got to dash. See you later! Thanks again, Tansy!'

1.15 p.m.

Still in the cafeteria. Eating doughnuts

'If you eat that stuff, you'll ruin your figure!' Allegra Webb swanned over to the table and perched on the end beside her cousin Jade, smoothing her skirt over her non-existent stomach to prove her point. 'I just had fruit.'

'I know,' observed Holly, winking at Jade. 'Half of it is stuck between your teeth!'

'What? It's not! Oh my God!' Allegra whipped a folding mirror out of her school bag and began scanning her reflection. 'I can't see –'

'She's teasing!' grinned Jade.

'You lot are so immature!' Allegra snapped. 'That's the worst part of being in Year Ten all over again – I have to mix with such juveniles!'

'And we,' murmured Holly, 'have to suffer such prima donnas!'

Allegra ignored her.

'Anyway, listen!' she went on. 'I need your advice. It's about this guy in Year Eleven ...'

'I might have guessed,' sighed Jade. 'Who is it this week?'

'Well, that's the whole point,' stressed Allegra. 'I don't know his name. But that's him, over there by the drinks machine.'

Jade, Holly and Tansy followed her gaze.

'Allegra,' sighed Tansy, 'there are at least seven guys by the drinks machine.'

'The tall one – with the blond hair,' sighed Allegra. 'He is to die for.'

'Warren Hudson,' said Holly. 'You're out of luck. He's got a girlfriend.'

'And,' grinned Allegra, 'if I've got anything to do with it, he's about to get a new one! Cheers, guys!'

She jumped down from the table, ran her fingers through her hair, and strolled towards the drinks cabinet.

'I thought she was going out with Hugo?' queried Tansy.

'He dumped her,' Jade replied. 'Said he didn't fancy being associated with a comprehensive school girl.'

'I don't believe it!' Holly gasped.

'You would if you'd met him,' commented Jade. 'He's a real snob. Trouble is, ever since, Legs has been desperate to get a new boyfriend. Can't think why.'

'I can,' sighed Holly. 'You need a guy in your life to feel complete.'

'That,' retorted Tansy, 'is what my mother thinks. And look at the mess it's got her into.'

1.25 p.m.

Making connections

At last! Cleo ran up the hill, praying that no teacher would spot that she was off the school site. Luckily the newsagent had had the right phone card and she had managed to call the phone company, key in her number and get them to credit her with loads of lovely units.

Now all she had to do was phone Trig.

She glanced at her watch. Right now, it was 7.25 in the morning in Illinois and Trig would be awake. She couldn't wait – once he got to school, he had to switch off his phone and she'd be back to square one.

She ran through the school gates, across the yard and behind the Art block. Leaning against the wall, she speed-dialled Trig's number.

'Come on, come on!' She willed him to answer.

'Hi!'

Cleo's heart somersaulted with joy.

'Trig! Darling, it's me, Cleo. What happened? Where were you?'

There was muffled muttering at the other end and Cleo strained her ears to catch what was said.

'Sorry, I couldn't hear. What did you say?'

'I was kinda tied up over the weekend,' Trig replied.

'Doing what?' Take an interest in a guy's activities, that's what all the books on love and relationships told you to do.

'This 'n' that,' he mumbled.

There was another rustling in the background.

'Say, I've got to go now – early session in school.'

'Wait!'

She swallowed hard.

'Trig?'

'Yeah?'

'You do still love me, don't you? You do still miss me?'

There was a pause.

'Sure I do,' came the reply.

'When will you phone me again?'

Another pause.

'Tomorrow,' he said. 'But I can't do it till after school —
it'll be eleven o'clock in the evening, your time, OK?'

'Brilliant,' she breathed. 'Can't wait. Love you!'

She waited for his reply, but all she heard was a click.

Lost the signal, she told herself. After all, America is a
long way away.

It was easier to believe that. Much easier than
wondering, just for an instant, whether Trig had actually
hung up on her.

3.45 p.m.

Walking home. Trying hard to feel in love

'I've hardly seen you all day,' complained Scott, taking
Jade's hand. 'I hate it now that we're in separate classes,
don't you?'

'Mmm,' murmured Jade. 'Still, we ...'

'Hey, you two! Wait for me!' Jade turned to see Allegra
belting down the hill after them.

'Oh no! Get rid of her, can't you?' pleaded Scott. 'I
want you to myself.'

'I can hardly do that,' reasoned Jade. 'We do live in the same house, after all.'

'You could if you wanted to!' retorted Scott. 'Are you avoiding –'

Jade was saved from having to answer by Allegra, who hurtled up to them and grabbed Jade's arm.

'Hi! Listen, that guy – Warren – who is he going out with?'

'Ursula Newley,' replied Jade.

'Ursula?' repeated Scott. 'But I thought she was going out with Alex.'

'That was last month,' observed Jade, as they crossed the road. 'Ursula changes boyfriends like most people change their underwear.'

'That's good!' declared Allegra. 'Because she's about to need a new one.'

Scott frowned.

'What do you mean?'

Allegra grinned.

'I got talking to Warren ...' she began.

'You mean,' corrected Jade, 'that you pinned him into a corner and started your three-minute chat-up routine. I know you.'

'Whatever!' Allegra waved a hand dismissively at Jade. 'Anyway, he said he was going to watch Dunchester Town playing in the League replay tonight, and I said that I adored football and –'

'You said WHAT?' Jade exploded. 'You hate football. Getting out of bed is usually too much exercise for you!'

'Stop being so picky!' ordered Allegra. 'Anyway, Warren said that he thought it was cool that a girl should like footie, because his girlfriend sulked every time he took time out to follow the team. And I said –'

'You said,' sighed Jade, 'that you couldn't imagine how any girl could be so selfish, and that if it was you, you'd support him every inch of the way.'

'How did you know?' demanded Allegra, slowing down at the corner of Dulverton Crescent.

'Let's just say it was an informed guess,' remarked Jade.

'So the thing is – I have to be at the match,' said Allegra. 'And I want you to come with me.'

'No way!' Jade shook her head. 'I've got better things to do.'

'Like what?' demanded her cousin.

'Like writing a history essay, and washing my hair and phoning my gran and ...'

Scott stared at her and stopped walking.

'And the family outing,' he said softly.

Jade's heart lurched. She'd forgotten the excuse she had given him earlier.

'... And that as well,' she finished lamely.

'Outing? What outing?' demanded Allegra.

'You know,' said Jade brightly, winking at Allegra with the eye furthest away from Scott, 'Helen's treat. Pizza and bowling?'

'What are you on about? She had a birthday treat last month ...'

'Oh, Legs, you're hopeless!' Jade tried to laugh and kick Allegra in the shins at the same time. 'Paula told us at the weekend. You'd forget your own head if it wasn't screwed on.'

'Well, Helen won't need me there, will she? What eight-year-old wants her big sister tagging along? I'm going to the football.'

'What about you, Jade?' murmured Scott. 'Are you still going with Helen?'

'Of course!' Jade tried to make her voice sound as natural as possible. 'I promised. I can't let her down.'

'Lucky Helen,' muttered Scott. 'I'll see you tomorrow.'

And with that, he crossed the road and headed for his house.

'Well, thanks a bunch!' Jade snapped, turning to Allegra. 'You could have gone along with my story. You dropped me in it big time.'

Allegra frowned.

'What do you mean?'

'I'd told Scott I couldn't see him tonight because Helen had a treat.'

'And I was supposed to read your mind?' questioned Allegra. 'Anyway, why wouldn't you see him?'

'Because ... it's just that lately ... oh, I don't know. Don't take any notice of me!'

'OK!' grinned Allegra. 'Now, what does one wear to a football match?'

4.10 p.m.

3 Plough Cottages. Facing a culinary surprise

Tansy pushed open the back door and stopped dead in her tracks. The kitchen table was piled high with food – and at least half of it looked edible. There was a large bowl of rice salad, a huge plate of sausages on sticks and a gooey-looking chocolate cake.

'Darling! You're back!' Tansy's mum flung open her

arms and hugged Tansy with as much enthusiasm as if she had just returned safely from a polar expedition. 'I thought we would have a bit of a treat.'

Tansy's brain went on red alert. Something was up. Her mother didn't do proper food – she served up organic vegetables and strange bits of greenery that should have been left growing in the hedgerows where they belonged. As for producing anything that had even looked at an E number or food colouring – that only happened at parties when Tansy really put her foot down.

'What's all this about?' demanded Tansy, gesturing towards the table.

'Well,' began her mother, swallowing hard and fiddling with her necklace, 'Henry's going to pop round.'

That, thought Tansy, is enough to put even the hungriest person off their food. Perhaps she could just eat now and disappear.

'What time is he coming?' demanded Tansy.

'Any minute now!' replied her mother cheerfully. 'We've got things to tell you and –'

'You've told me quite enough already!' exploded Tansy. 'And besides ...'

She stopped.

And stared at her mother's left hand.

'What's that?' she whispered, even though she knew quite well what it was.

'Isn't it lovely?' breathed her mother, stretching out her hand so that Tansy could see the sapphire and diamond ring glinting on her fourth finger. 'Henry brought it round this morning. It's my engagement ring.'

Tansy's heart lurched. So it was really happening. Her mother hadn't changed her mind.

'It's antique!' her mother went on proudly.

'Probably made when Henry was born then,' muttered Tansy, turning away and stomping through the sitting room to the stairs. The ring was beautiful, but she wasn't going to admire it. She wasn't going to accept anything that was remotely connected with Henry Fazackerley.

Not now.

Not ever.

4.45 p.m.

In her bedroom at 6 Kestrel Close. Dreaming

Twenty-nine hours and fifteen minutes. She would be talking to Trig in just twenty-nine hours and fifteen minutes. It seemed like a lifetime, Cleo thought, but at least he had promised to call, which meant that he was finding the separation as harrowing as she was. And she was sure there was a simple explanation for his silence; probably his computer had gone on the blink and he couldn't send e-mails. Computers were so unreliable.

That would be it.

Tomorrow night he would tell her how much he missed her.

And she would tell him that she couldn't live without him.

And everything would be all right.

5.05 p.m.

'I can't, Henry! I simply can't do that!'

Tansy's heart leapt and she flung her homework to one side and ran out on to the landing. Her mum had seen sense! She had realized she couldn't marry Henry. Oh joy.

'What do you mean, you can't? Of course you can! It's all arranged!'

'But, Henry! I mean, it's a lovely idea but it's imposs-ible ...'

Too right it is, thought Tansy, edging her way down the stairs in order to hear better.

'Impossible? Nothing's impossible for Henry Fazackerley! And just think how exciting it will be!'

'Well, I know – it would be amazing but how can we ...?'

She was weakening! She couldn't give in now.

'Go on – you know you want to really!' she heard Henry cajole. 'Say yes!'

There was a long pause and Tansy held her breath until she thought her lungs would burst.

'All right then ... YES!' Her mother sounded triumphant and not at all like a woman who had been coerced into doing something she didn't want to do.

'If my mum doesn't want to marry you, she doesn't have to!' Tansy burst into the kitchen and glared at Henry. 'And nothing you can say will make her change –'

'Tansy!'

Her mother, far from appearing grateful for her intervention, looked positively irate.

'Oh, she wants to marry me, all right, don't you, my

little eggnog?' asked Henry, wrapping a proprietorial arm around Tansy's mother.

Oh please! thought Tansy, wincing at Henry's sugary tones.

'Of course I do!' Her mother looked up at her fiancé with adoring eyes.

'Aren't you going to congratulate me, Tansy, on winning over your wonderful mum?'

'No!' Tansy knew she sounded surly, but she honestly couldn't help it.

'Oh, Tansy ...' Tansy thought her mum looked rather nervous, but then the sight of Henry's hairy chest poking through an open-necked shirt adorned with a badge that read 'Hunky Hip Hellraiser!' was enough to make anyone anxious.

'Should I tell her what you've just suggested?' Clarity sounded as if she wouldn't make a cup of tea without Henry's approval.

'Not suggested, my little funky fishcake – arranged!'

Tansy thought she might vomit.

'What now?' she asked, eyeing the chocolate cake and wondering whether she would lose ground by pausing to cut a slice.

Clarity gave a little cough.

'Well, the thing is, you know that Saturday is my birthday?'

'Yes,' murmured Tansy.

'So,' Clarity cried, 'we are going to be married on Saturday!'

'SATURDAY?' Tansy gasped. 'You don't mean this Saturday?'

'Yes, darling – isn't that the most wonderful birthday

surprise ever! Henry had it all planned ...'

'But you can't!' Tansy shouted. 'Anyway, you couldn't possibly get it organized in time!'

Henry threw back his head and roared with laughter. Tansy watched his Adam's apple jigging up and down and wanted to strangle him.

'Ah, but you've reckoned without me!' he cried. 'I booked the registrar just two weeks after I met your mum. Henry Fazackerley is not a chap to let the grass grow under his feet.'

Clarity gazed at him lovingly.

'He knew, didn't you, Henry?' she murmured. 'He just knew that Destiny had brought us together and that we were meant for one another.'

Tansy stared at them.

'I don't believe this is happening,' she whispered.

'Well, you had better believe it!' cried Henry. 'Because in just five days' time, I'll be your new stepdad. Now what do you say to that?'

Tansy wanted to cry, but she wasn't going to give either of them the satisfaction.

'I've been brought up not to swear,' she snarled, pushing all thoughts of chocolate cake from her mind and turning away. 'So I won't say anything if you don't mind!'

And with that, she ran from the room.

And only then did she let herself burst into tears.

6 p.m.

The Cedars, Weston Way. Attempting the impossible

'Clarity? Getting married? Are you sure?' Holly's mother eyed her in disbelief.

'Of course I'm sure,' replied Holly. 'Tansy told me and she's dead upset about it.'

'But this Henry – I've never met him!' Her mother sounded peeved.

'I don't imagine,' replied Holly, 'that Tansy's mum thought of asking your permission. Anyway, you have to put her off him.'

Holly's mum raised her eyes.

'Darling, I can't do that – it's none of my business.'

'Well, you'll have to make it your business,' stressed Holly. 'This is an emergency. Tansy could be traumatized for life.'

'Knowing Tansy,' retorted her mother dryly, 'I doubt it. I think that young lady is perfectly capable of looking after herself.'

'In that case,' replied Holly loftily, 'you have even less understanding of teenagers than I thought.'

7 p.m.

53 Lime Avenue, Oak Hill. In the bedroom

'You can't go to a football match looking like that!' objected Jade, surveying Allegra's micro mini skirt and cropped top. 'You'll die of cold.'

'God, you sound just like my mother!' retorted Allegra. 'Now then, do these shoes make my ankles look alluring?'

'They make you look like you're about to fall over!' grinned Jade. 'Besides, it'll be dark – Warren won't see much.'

'Oh yes he will!' retorted Allegra. 'I'll make sure of that. This could be the start of something very big.'

'Like pneumonia,' replied Jade. 'Good luck.'

7.10 p.m.

The hour of reckoning

'Right, Cleo! Over here!' Her stepfather looked up from the kitchen table where he was scribbling figures on a sheet of paper. 'You owe me fifty-seven pounds for phone calls.'

'WHAT?' Cleo's eyes widened and she snatched the paper. 'That can't be right!'

'Believe me, it is,' Roy remarked. 'And I've been generous – I have only charged you for the American calls. I've ignored all your chattering to your school friends.'

He eyed her triumphantly.

'And the telecom company have barred all international calls from this number! So … let's be having the cash.'

'I haven't got that much!' said Cleo.

'So give me what you have got and then get the rest from your building society,' Roy said tersely. 'I'm doing it for your own good. I don't want you turning out to be a spendthrift like your mother.'

'There's nothing wrong with my mother!' spat Cleo. 'At least she's not a tight-fisted, mean –'

'Just get the money,' sighed her stepfather.

So much, thought Cleo, for her mother getting him sorted!

7.20 p.m.

Being interrupted

'Can I come in?' Tansy's mum knocked lightly on her bedroom door.

'If you must.'

Clarity kissed the top of Tansy's head and perched on the end of her bed.

'Look, darling,' she began, 'I know this has been a bit of a shock for you but I know that given time, you'll get used to it and –'

'Dream on!'

'But, Tansy, you used to say that Henry made you laugh and ...'

It was true. She had found Henry a bit of a giggle with his hippy ways and daft way of talking. But that was before she realized he had serious designs on her mother.

'Homer Simpson makes me laugh,' she told Clarity, 'but I wouldn't want you to marry him!'

She knew she was being stroppy but she couldn't help herself.

Her mother tried again.

'Anyway, I want you to help me plan the wedding!' she continued brightly. 'I want something really special, a day to remember –'

'Oh my God!' Tansy clamped a hand to her mouth.

'What?'

'Henry will be living here, won't he? All the time? And sleeping in your bedroom!'

Her mother laughed.

'Well, of course!' she replied. 'That's what married people do.' She eyed Tansy nervously. 'Actually,' she murmured, 'he's moving in tomorrow.'

'Oh yuk!' sighed Tansy. 'I don't suppose you fancy buying me a flat, do you? Like now?'

Three minutes later

'What does Henry do, exactly?' Tansy asked.

'He used to own a nursery,' her mother replied.

'Children or flowers?'

'Flowers, silly,' laughed her mother. 'But he sold it, made a tidy little profit and now he's retired.'

'Retired?' Tansy made it sound as if he was a carrier of the bubonic plague. 'But that means he'll be under your feet all day every day!'

Work on this one, she thought. Put her off big time.

'You'll hate that, Mum! I mean, this cottage is very small and ...'

Clarity smiled.

'Next year, he's going to buy me my very own nursery and we will run it together. He's even going to open a joint account after the wedding and put money in for me! Isn't that wonderful?'

'Mind-blowing,' sighed Tansy.

'So – you will help me, won't you, darling? Plan the wedding, I mean? I've never been married and I do so want it to be lovely.'

Tansy looked at her mother. Her cheeks were flushed pink and her eyes were dancing. She looked really pretty.

And happy.

And ten years younger.

Suddenly Tansy felt even more muddled than before. She wanted her mum to be happy – but she didn't want Henry to be the one to make her that way.

On the other hand, she didn't want to spoil everything for her mother. After all, in four years' time she could leave home.

Or two, if it really got dire.

'OK,' she said, trying to smile. 'I'll help.'

Her mother smothered her in kisses.

'Thank you, darling!' she cried. 'I'm so happy … and you see – you will be too. I promise. Now – come and eat!'

'I can't eat – I'm far too traumatized,' replied Tansy.

'Pity,' sighed Clarity, 'because I bought some Chunky Monkey ice cream today.'

'On the other hand,' mused Tansy, 'I suppose I ought to keep my strength up.'

8.15 p.m.

Spreading the news

'And what's more, he eats like a pig and he's moving in tomorrow!' Tansy had been on the phone to Holly for over ten minutes, listing Henry's failings. 'Holly, what am I going to do? I mean, she's marrying him on Saturday and –'

'We have to launch a campaign,' Holly declared.

'Oh yeah, right!' muttered Tansy. 'Like that's going to change things overnight.'

'Don't be defeatist!' ordered Holly. 'Leave it with me. By tomorrow, I'll have a whole load of ideas.'

'Really?'

'Trust me,' said Holly. 'I'm awesome when roused.'

TUESDAY

7.45 a.m.

Post-mortem on the footie

'So how was the football?' Jade asked Allegra as they vied for space at the mirror. 'Or more to the point, how was Warren?'

'Don't talk to me about Warren Hudson!' spat Allegra, scooping her hair up in a glitzy hairslide.

'That good?' grinned Jade.

'To start with, it took me ages to find him. He wasn't in any of the seats ...'

'Legs, guys stand at footie matches and –'

'Yes, well, I didn't know that, and then when I did find him, he was with a huge crowd of his mates and he hardly said a word. And it was freezing cold and boring and I've had it with boys!'

'You? Had it with boys? You'll be telling me next that the moon is made of green cheese!'

Jade expected Allegra to come back with some witty reply but instead, she looked close to tears.

'I do miss Hugo,' she whispered. 'I loved him so much and he loved me and –'

'Get real!' retorted Jade firmly. 'The only person Hugo loved was Hugo – you deserve better!'

'It's all right for you,' Allegra sighed. 'You have Scott. He's so sweet.'

Jade said nothing. It was true, Scott was a darling. Only not the darling for her. Not any more.

The trouble was, she didn't have the heart to tell him so.

And she didn't have the energy to go on pretending.

There were times when being half of a couple was more effort than it was worth.

8 a.m.

In the kitchen, being confused

'I thought something medieval,' remarked Tansy's mum as Tansy stuffed the remains of the chocolate cake into her lunch box. 'Or then again, Grecian. But medieval would be more appropriate, don't you think, darling?'

Tansy eyed her mother wearily.

'Mum,' she sighed. 'What are you on about?'

'My outfit, sweetheart,' Clarity explained. 'For the wedding. I do want to dress in keeping with the surroundings.'

'Dunchester Registry Office is hardly the Ritz,' replied Tansy. 'I remember when Cleo's mum got married –'

'But darling, didn't I say?' enthused Clarity. 'We're not going to the Registry Office – boring! We're being married in the ruins of Dunchester Castle.'

'WHAT?' Tansy gasped. 'You are going to do it in full view of the general public?'

'It was Henry's idea,' beamed her mother.

'I might have guessed,' sighed Tansy. 'And you agreed?'

'Of course I did! It's so romantic!'

'It's insane!

She caught sight of her mother's crestfallen expression.

'But I do love you,' she grinned, giving her a hug. 'Dottiness and all.'

8.05 a.m.

Parenting the parent. Again

Only fourteen hours and twenty-five minutes to go before Trig calls, thought Cleo, running down the stairs and along the hall. She felt so happy that her appetite had decided to make up for lost time, and she pushed open the kitchen door, and headed straight for the cupboards.

'Mum, did I tell you that Tansy's mum ... Mum! What's wrong?'

Diana was sitting at the kitchen table, head in hands, and her shoulders were shaking.

'Mum, you're crying! What is it? What's happened?'

Diana sniffed hastily and tried to smile.

'Nothing,' she said.

'Come off it, Mum,' replied Cleo. 'Tell me.'

'Just PMT,' her mother said, and then pulled a pile of envelopes towards her.

'And these,' she added dully.

Cleo peered over her shoulder.

And gasped.

'*Barclaycard, Access, Diners Club,*' she read. 'Mum – these are huge! One thousand five hundred and sixty pounds, one thousand eight hundred and ninety-six pounds ... what's going on?'

'I didn't mean to spend this much,' her mother sighed. 'It just sort of mounted up. And then this came.'

She shoved another sheet of paper in Cleo's direction.

'It's from a debt-collection company,' she explained miserably. 'If I don't pay, they'll take me to court.'

'So pay,' advised Cleo.

'I can't,' her mother said softly. 'I haven't got the money.'

Cleo stared at her.

'But what about the money from the TV advert ... ?'

'Gone,' murmured her mother. 'But,' she added, brightening, 'I phoned my agent and she said she's sure that my big break is just round the corner and then, of course, everything will be paid off in next to no time!'

She sat up, looking a lot happier.

'Now what were you going to tell me?'

'Tansy's mum is getting married,' announced Cleo.

'Darling!' Diana cried. 'How wonderful!'

'No it's not,' Cleo corrected her. 'It's hideous. She's marrying this guy Henry who is ancient and really weird and –'

'When did you meet him?'

'I haven't.'

'So,' ordered her mother, 'you shouldn't make judgements about people you don't know. He's probably delightful.'

'Tansy hates him,' Cleo told her.

'That,' said her mother, 'has nothing to do with it. You loathed Roy when you first met him.'

Cleo said nothing.

It was wiser that way.

8.15 a.m.

Calling for Andy

'Sorry I'm early,' said Tansy when Andy opened the front door. 'My mother was driving me crazy with ... what on earth is that noise?'

The sound of scraping and thudding and banging echoed down the stairs.

'That,' sighed Andy, 'is my mum getting ready for the twins.'

Tansy grinned.

'What's she doing – hand carving a couple of cots?'

'Turning MY bedroom into a nursery,' he replied. 'She turfed me out last night and started scraping off the wallpaper at about five o'clock this morning. I think pregnancy has sent her round the bend.'

'Oh no it hasn't!' Mrs Richards appeared at the top of the stairs, dressed in denim dungarees and with her hair tied up in a scarf. 'Hi, Tansy!'

'Hello,' said Tansy, trying very hard not to stare at Mrs Richards' vast stomach. 'How are you?'

'Fat, breathless and being kicked from all sides,' Andy's mother replied cheerfully.

'You shouldn't be doing all that decorating,'commented Andy. 'Pregnant women are supposed to rest.'

His mum roared with laughter.

'Oh, and you're a world expert, are you, darling? Besides, the babies aren't due for ages – I've got two more months to go!'

She patted her tummy affectionately and turned to Tansy.

'By the way, is it true what Andy tells me? That your mum is getting married?'

Tansy nodded.

"Fraid so,' she said.

'How lovely!' Mrs Richards clapped her hands in delight and almost dug her own eye out with the scraper. 'I must phone her – I need some advice.'

'You want advice from my mother?' queried Tansy.

'I do.'

'Your mum,' she grinned at Andy, 'is clearly not a well woman.'

9.40 a.m.

In the kitchen at The Cedars. On the phone

'Clarity? Angela Vine here! I just wanted to congratulate you. Holly told me about your engagement.'

Angela perched on the kitchen table and smoothed her ancient cord skirt over her knees.

'But do tell me – I'm sure that Holly has it all wrong – she mentioned something about Saturday ... it is Saturday?' She gulped. 'And we're invited? How lovely!'

Oh heck, she thought.

11 a.m.

At break having a crisis conference

'On Saturday?' Jade gasped.

'This Saturday?' queried Cleo.

'So that's that then,' concluded Andy.

'I guess,' sighed Tansy.

'Just a minute, you lot!' objected Holly. 'What's with all this giving up? There's loads of things we can do.'

'Like what?' demanded Tansy.

'You could get ill,' suggested Holly. 'Badly ill and then she'd have to cancel the wedding and –'

'Excuse me,' interrupted Tansy, 'but I can't just fall sick at the drop of a hat.'

'You could pretend,' suggested Jade.

Tansy raised an eyebrow.

'No, silly idea,' sighed Jade.

'Couldn't you just make the most of it?' intervened Cleo. 'I mean, I had to with Roy.'

'Roy,' said Tansy, 'is normal.'

'You don't live with him!' retorted Cleo. 'My grandmother says he's –'

'Grandmother!' Tansy gasped 'That's it!'

They all looked at her in amazement.

'My gran – she doesn't know yet. She doesn't approve of anything Mum does, on principle.'

'Brilliant!' cried Holly. 'Phone her and tell her and then wait for the fireworks!'

'I'm not being funny,' began Andy, 'but what difference will it make? Your mum's an adult – she won't be scared of her own mother.'

'You,' said Tansy dryly, 'haven't met my gran.'

12.15 p.m.

Making plans

Not now, thought Cleo's mother as the telephone shrilled at the end of the hall. She had just twenty minutes to get to the bank and try to persuade the manager to give her a lovely big loan to pay off her credit cards. She couldn't be late. It wouldn't look good.

'Hello? Diana Greenway here! ... Oh, Clarity! Hello, darling! Sweetheart, the bestest congratulations! What a dark horse you are!'

She glanced at her watch as Tansy's mother launched into a long explanation about the love of her life.

'Darling, I have to dash ... what's that? Me? Help you choose an outfit? Oh, I'd love to ... Yes, yes I am awfully good at that sort of thing, aren't I?'

She grabbed her organizer from her handbag.

'Tomorrow? Ten o'clock? Shall we meet outside Doyles? It's such a lovely shop – you know, Armani, Jean Muir, that wonderful Ghost stuff ... what's that?'

She sneaked another peek at her watch.

'Oh darling, of course I will! You're right! I shall apply my little grey brain cells to the idea right now! Oh we will have fun! See you then! Ciao!'

She banged the receiver down and opened the front door.

What fun! An exotic outfit for Clarity to get sorted – and

then of course, she'd need something new. Not expensive of course – but beautifully cut. She did have good hips for her age, even if she said so herself.

She felt better already.

12.40 p.m.

Matters financial

'Cleo, can I have my ten pounds back?' Tansy dumped her jacket potato and baked beans on the table and looked expectantly at her friend.

'Ah,' said Cleo, gazing closely at her chicken pie.

'What do you mean, "ah"?' demanded Tansy.

'I haven't got it,' admitted Cleo.

'Cleo!' Tansy snapped. 'You promised! I've got to get Mum's birthday pressie.'

'I'll bring it tomorrow,' Cleo assured her.

'And my one pound fifty, if you don't mind!' added Holly.

'OK, OK,' murmured Cleo. And begun wondering how to ask her mum for more money.

1 p.m.

Ringing the wrinkly

'OK, so phone your gran,' ordered Jade. 'Sound really anxious and depressed. It makes grandmothers go all protective.'

'Not when they are dead ringers for Cruella De Vil, it doesn't!' retorted Tansy.

She dialled her gran's number.

It rang for ages.

'Yes?'

'Hi, Gran, it's me!' Tansy tried to sound like the perfect loving grandchild. 'Tansy! ... No, not the taxi. Tansy.'

'Oh you,' she heard her grandmother remark. 'I'm just about to go out. What do you want?'

Tansy swallowed. So much for 'How lovely to hear your voice, darling!'

'It's about Mum,' she began.

'Is she ill?' For a second, her gran sounded anxious.

'No, she's fine ... only, she's getting married.'

'She's what?'

'Getting married, Gran. To this really old, very peculiar man.'

'Your mother only goes around with peculiar men!' retorted her grandmother. 'She never did have any taste!'

She sniffed so loudly that Jade, who was listening in, could hardly stifle her giggles.

'Mind you,' added Tansy's grandmother, 'most men are peculiar, if you ask me.'

'Gran, you have to stop her!' Tansy urged. 'She'll listen to you.'

As if.

'No she won't, she never listens to me. Look what happened last time. She got in with the wrong sort and you turned up.'

She made it sound as though Tansy had arrived on a number seventeen bus.

'Not,' added her grandmother, 'that you haven't turned out all right, I'm not saying that but –'

'Gran! Listen! She's doing it on Saturday!'

'Doing what on Saturday?'

Honestly, thought Tansy, what was it with old people?

'Marrying Henry. In the castle ruins.'

'How utterly ridiculous,' cried her grandmother. 'She'll get mud on her shoes.'

Complete madness, thought Tansy. That was the only explanation.

'And why haven't I had an invitation?' her grandmother demanded.

'No one has yet,' Tansy told her. 'Not even Beth.'

'Huh!' grunted her gran.

'Please, Gran, talk to Mum. Please.'

There was a long pause.

'I'll come down,' her grandmother informed her. 'Not tomorrow – that's my bridge day and the cat's having her injections. Expect me on Thursday. Dunchester East. Four thirty-five.'

'But ...' Tansy began. Getting her gran to talk to her mother was one thing; having her to stay was quite another. She'd expect to have Tansy's room and no way was she spending the night on the sofa.

'And I won't stay in your place,' her gran announced. 'I shall take a room at The Beaufort. I like the Eggs Benedict.'

There was a click, and she was gone.

Tansy gaped at Jade.

'She's coming down. From Scotland. The day after tomorrow.'

'That's great!' cried Jade. 'Well done you!'

'I think,' sighed Tansy, 'that I've just made things a whole heap worse.'

4.15 p.m.

3 Plough Cottages. Embarrassment overload

'Oh no!' Tansy stopped dead in her tracks as she and Andy turned the corner into Cattle Hill. 'Henry's here!'

She pointed up the road to where a bright pink Cadillac was parked outside her cottage.

'That's Henry's car?' Andy gasped. 'That is like so totally cool!'

'It's hideous!' retorted Tansy. 'It's so ... in your face.'

'You said last week that you'd rather drive around in a Skoda than in your mum's pick-up truck!' Andy reminded her. 'And that –' He gestured at the Cadillac – 'is certainly no Skoda! This Henry must be quite a guy!'

'Honestly!' snapped Tansy. 'What is it with males? Just because you like the car you assume the man must be great. Well, come in and meet him. That'll soon put you straight!'

'Will it be all right?' Andy asked.

'Sure,' said Tansy. 'And what's more it puts off the time when I have to tell my mother that Gran is arriving on Thursday. I don't somehow think she's going to be very happy.'

She flung open the back gate, stomped across the gravel and through the back door into the kitchen. Her mother was sitting at the kitchen table, surrounded by sheets of paper and Henry was perched on the counter top. He was wearing combat trousers and a fluorescent orange T-shirt with the words 'Groovy Guy' emblazoned across it. His long grey hair was tied back in a ponytail with what looked like a chewed shoelace. He looked like a badly drawn cartoon.

'Here she is!' boomed Henry, leaping to his feet. 'The little lady herself!'

Tansy glowered at him.

'Darling, I'm so glad you're back!' beamed Clarity. 'I need your ... oh, Andy, I didn't see you there! How are you?'

'Fine, thanks!' smiled Andy.

'Andy is Tansy's boyfriend,' Clarity said, turning to Henry. 'He's a lovely lad, aren't you, Andy? I must say I never thought Tansy would take up with anyone quite as sensible as –'

'MUM!' Tansy resisted the urge to throttle her mother.

'Congratulations on your gorgeous girlfriend, old chum!' cried Henry, giving Andy a nudge that almost sent him flying across the ktichen. 'Like mother, like daughter, eh? Wow!'

'I like your car, sir!' Andy interrupted, his face colouring as he eyed Henry up and down.

'You don't have to call him sir!' hissed Tansy.

'Great, isn't she?' enthused Henry. 'Purrs like a pussy cat – bit like your mum, eh, Tansy?'

'Henry!' Now even Clarity looked embarrassed. 'How's your mum, Andy?'

'Decorating,' sighed Andy. 'And making cakes.'

'Nest-building,' said Clarity in satisfaction. 'But it's ages until the babies are due, isn't it?'

Andy nodded.

'Still, I get to have cake every night,' he grinned. 'She's baking like a maniac.'

'Is she now?' Clarity looked thoughtful. 'Would she

make a cake for me, do you think?'

Before Andy could answer, Henry slapped him on the back and nearly knocked him over.

'Wedding for the use of,' he boomed. 'Tell your mum we want something way out and wacky, isn't that right, my little tiddley pussycat?'

He tickled Clarity's nose and she giggled like a six-year-old.

'I'll ask,' said Andy hastily, throwing a bemused glance in Tansy's direction. 'Better go. Homework and stuff.'

Tansy walked with him to the back gate.

'So?' Tansy asked. 'What do you think? Would you want that as a stepfather?'

Andy sighed.

'No way!' he replied. 'In fact, yelling babies suddenly seem a doddle compared with living with him!'

He frowned.

'You know, he reminds me of someone – I can't think who.'

'Frankenstein's monster? Attila the Hun?'

Andy shook his head.

'Maybe it's someone on TV. Anyway, he's pretty weird. You'll have to do something.'

'Tell me about it,' replied Tansy. 'The problem is – what?'

Ten minutes later

'Right, darling, now listen,' ordered Clarity, scribbling on a sheet of paper. 'We've been making a guest list – of course, I'll have to phone everyone, there's no time for printed invitations.'

She picked up a list.

'You, me, Henry,' she began.

'Where is Henry?' asked Tansy.

'Upstairs making a few phone calls,' said her mum. 'Between you and me, I think he's got a few more surprises up his sleeve for the wedding.'

Tansy groaned.

'Every time his mobile rings, he winks at me and scuttles out of earshot!' she giggled. 'He is a dear.'

Tansy bit her tongue.

'So what about this guest list?' she urged.

'Oh yes! I thought Angela and Rupert Vine, and Holly, of course, to keep you company, and the Greenways because Diana's helping with the outfits and Val, of course, and Andy and Jade's family because I think they might be putting some gardening work my way and ...'

She paused and frowned at Tansy.

'Now when are we going to get your bridesmaid's dress?'

'My WHAT?' Tansy cried

'Bridesmaid's dress, darling,' her mother enthused. 'I've had this amazing idea for a theme to the wedding and –'

'Mum, I am not being a bridesmaid. Absolutely, categorically and definitely not. OK?'

Clarity looked crestfallen.

'But, darling, you're my daughter. I want the day to be really special for you too.'

'Then cancel it!' spat Tansy and hurtled out of the room.

Another ten minutes later

She shouldn't have said that. It was mean, she knew it was. And now she could hear her mum sobbing in the kitchen and Henry trying to soothe her.

'Just a self-centred kid ... they're all the same ... deserves a real rollicking ... if she was mine ... I'll have a word with her.'

No way. She wouldn't give him the satisfaction.

Slowly, she went downstairs and into the kitchen.

She took a deep breath.

'I'm sorry, Mum,' she said. 'I shouldn't have said that. It was mean.'

Clarity looked up, her eyes pink and moist, and nodded.

'So – will you be my bridesmaid?'

'Of course she won't!' Henry butted in. 'She's a typical teenager ...'

That did it.

'Sure, Mum, of course I will!' she smiled, giving her mother a hug. 'Whatever you want.'

Her mum squeezed her hand.

'I'm so pleased,' she said. 'I was thinking of apricot chiffon.'

Tansy opened her mouth.

And shut it again.

She knew when she had lost.

8 p.m.

Cleo loves Trig ... Cleopatra Roscoe, wife of the eminent archaeologist Trig Roscoe ... Cleo and Trig 4ever ...

Cleo tore the sheet of paper out of her homework folder and looked at her watch for the fifth time.

Exactly two hours to go. In two hours' time he would phone her.

And she would say such wonderful things to him – she would read a poem down the phone, and tell him that the miles between them were just like a piece of fluff to be blown away on the breeze. She'd read that in her mother's *Romance* magazine and thought it was quite perfect.

And so would he.

8.45 p.m.

'Has Henry gone?' asked Tansy, poking her head around the kitchen door.

Her mother nodded.

'Back to his lonely little flat,' she murmured. 'Poor lamb – still, it's not for much longer.'

Her mother sighed.

'Poor love, he's had such a sad life,' she mused. 'Do you know, there won't be one single person from his family at the wedding? Don't you think that's tragic?'

Tansy frowned.

'What about his kids?'

'Deborah lives in Australia, and Duncan's in South America,' her mother reminded her. 'They'd never get here on time.'

I guess if Henry was my dad, I'd move to the other side of the world too, thought Tansy.

'He has no one,' Clarity went on sadly. 'No brothers, no sisters ... so I told him that our family would be his family. Only there's just one thing ...'

'What?'

'I'm not telling Gran or Beth about the wedding until it's over,' she gabbled, averting her eyes. 'Gran will only spoil everything and if I invite Beth without inviting Gran, there will be all hell to pay. So I'm keeping quiet till after the event.'

'That's not going to work,' replied Tansy softly. 'Gran knows.'

Clarity's face paled.

'What?'

'I rang her,' confessed Tansy. 'I mean, I had to – you're doing such a crazy thing and ...'

Her voice tailed off.

'Tansy, how could you?' Her mother sounded shell-shocked.

'I'm sorry,' said Tansy. 'The thing is ...'

She hesitated.

'What?'

'She's coming down. On Thursday.'

'SHE IS WHAT?'

Clarity looked as if she might explode any moment.

'It's OK,' Tansy assured her hastily, 'she's not staying here ...'

'You're dead right she's not!'

'She's going to The Beaufort.'

Tansy nibbled a fingernail.

'I guess I should have phoned Beth instead but ...'

'You shouldn't have phoned anyone!' shouted her mother. 'You should have minded your own business. Are you determined to spoil everything for me?'

'No, but –'

'Just go away, Tansy! Just leave me alone!'

Tansy opened her mouth to protest and then shut it again. What was the point?

It wasn't until she was upstairs in her bedroom that

a thought struck her.

If her mother was so certain that Henry really was the guy for her, why was she keeping him a secret from her mother and only sister?

11 p.m.

The tension mounts

Cleo sat on the edge of her bed, watching the minute hand ticking its way round the watch face and clutching her mobile phone to her chest.

Any minute now.

Any minute now

11.10 p.m.

... and mounts

He was probably having trouble getting through. The networks would be buzzing. Maybe he had been kept in late at school. He was probably getting really frustrated

11.25 p.m.

... and mounts

She would count to one hundred in French and then in German and by then he would have rung.

11.35 p.m.

The heart sinks

He hadn't.

11.45 p.m.

... and sinks

He wasn't going to.

But he had promised.

Maybe the clocks had changed in America. Maybe there was an extra hour difference.

She would wait till midnight.

He was certain to have phoned by midnight.

Midnight. ...

and almost stops.

The knot in the pit of her stomach was getting bigger.

She would have to call him.

She speed-dialled his number.

The line was busy!

Her heart lifted. He was trying to call her.

She waited.

WEDNESDAY

12.10 a.m.

Cleo's hopes fade

And waited.

12.12 a.m.

... and vanish

There must be a fault on the line. She would phone him.
She dialled his home number.

It rang.

And rang.

And rang.

'The Roscoe house – hello?'

The voice was unfamiliar.

'Can I speak to Trig, please?'

Her mouth was so dry that she could hardly speak.

'Trig? You've just missed him. He's gone out for the
evening.'

Gone out?

'Can I take a message? It's his mother speaking.'

'Yes,' mumbled Cleo. 'Can you tell him Cleo called?'

'Chloë?'

'No, Cleo!' she shouted.

'Sure thing, Kylie!' said his mum.

'No, not Kylie ...'

'Thanks for calling. Have a good evening!'

Some hope, Cleo thought miserably, hurling her phone on to the bed.

Trig had gone out. Without phoning her. And his mum didn't even recognize her name.

Which meant he never talked about her.

He'd found someone else.

She just knew he had.

She flung herself face down on the bed and began to cry.

And once she had started, she found she simply couldn't stop.

7.30 a.m.

'Good grief!' Tansy burst into the kitchen and stared at her mother. 'Don't tell me you are dressing up just because Henry is coming for breakfast?'

Her mother laughed.

'He's not coming,' she said.

'God is good,' muttered Tansy.

'I'm going shopping with Diana for my wedding outfit,' she said. 'And your bridesmaids' clothes.'

Tansy said nothing.

'Aren't you excited?' pleaded her mother.

'Ecstatic,' sighed Tansy.

8 a.m.

Coping with maternal excesses

'But, Mum, you shouldn't be going shopping anyway!' Cleo protested, as she poured orange juice somewhat haphazardly into a glass. 'You can't afford it – you said so!'

'Oh, but darling,' her mother reasoned, 'I'm only going to help Clarity choose her dress. It won't be my money that she will be spending.'

Cleo yawned and looked at her pityingly.

'Mum,' she asked, 'when have you ever been into a shop and not spent money?'

'I'm a reformed woman,' her mother vowed. 'The bank manager says that once I've cleared my overdraft –'

'You've got an overdraft as well as all those credit card bills?' Cleo gasped.

This was a worry.

'Only a teeny one, darling, and anyway, once that's gone, he's going to give me a loan to pay off everything else. He's a sweet man, lovely little bum and –'

'Mum!' Cleo retorted. 'So – I don't suppose you can lend me ten pounds?'

'No,' said her mother.

Parents, thought Cleo, were hopeless when it came to priorities.

8.45 a.m.

In the schoolyard

'Allegra! Hang on a minute!' Scott moved away from the group of guys he had been talking to, and grabbed Allegra's arm. 'Where's Jade?'

Allegra brushed her hair out of her eyes.

'In the art block – she came early to finish her assignment,' she said.

'But we've got weeks before that has to be in!' protested Scott.

He rammed his hands into his pockets and sighed.

'I think she's avoiding me,' he muttered.

'Would it matter if she was?' asked Allegra.

Scott looked up in alarm.

'Of course it would matter!' he said. 'Are you saying that you know something? Is she avoiding me? Well, is she?'

Allegra shrugged her shoulders.

'How should I know?' she replied. 'I can't imagine why she would – you don't seem like the kind of guy any girl with any sense would ignore.'

She smiled sweetly, waved her hand and sauntered off.

It was always best to let a guy ponder on one's words for a bit.

And then go in for the kill.

8.55 a.m.

In the classroom waiting for registration

'Hey, careful!' Cleo stumbled against the doorpost as Scott pushed past, his face a picture of misery. 'What's the matter with you?'

'Nothing!' he snapped and stomped over to a corner table.

Oh sure, thought Cleo. Not that you are likely to have half the problems I've got. Your girlfriend is here in the same room, whereas your best mate, the guy I adore, is three thousand ... That was it! Why on earth hadn't she thought of it before? Scott was Trig's best mate. They had been joined at the hip when Trig was at West Green. Scott would be sure to know if something awful was happening in Trig's life.

'Scott!' she rushed up to him, anxious to get to him before Mr Grubb came in for Registration. 'Have you heard from Trig lately?'

Scott nodded.

'Sure,' he said.

'When? How?'

Scott turned away and looked out of the window.

'He phoned me last night.'

Cleo stared at him.

'Last night?' she repeated. 'You spoke to him last night?'

'Mmm.'

But he was meant to phone me last night. If he had time to call you, why not me?

'What did he say?' She held her breath. 'Is he OK?'

'Great,' Scott nodded. 'He's made loads of new friends at this school of his, and he's having a ball, going out nights and –'

'So, did he ...?' She stopped. She wanted to ask if Trig had mentioned her name. But if he hadn't, she didn't think she could bear to know. 'So if you speak to him again,' she said, her mouth so dry that she could hardly talk, 'can you tell him our phone is mended now? He won't have been able to get through lately.'

'OK,' he said. 'I'll tell him.'

But he didn't meet her eye.

10.30 a.m.

Dressing up

'Oh Clarity, this is such fun! Now, what about this one?'

Diana grabbed a hanger from the clothes rail and held it up in the air.

'It's frightfully you, darling!' she enthused. 'So sophisticated, don't you think?'

Clarity laughed.

'It might be, if my stomach was flatter and my hips narrower,' she commented. 'Diana, you don't think I'm being silly, do you?'

'What, marrying Henry? Well, darling, none of us know him that well, but as long as you're sure that Henry –'

'No, no, not marrying Henry!' interjected Clarity. 'I know he's right for me. I meant do you think I'm silly to want a really romantic wedding at my age? I've always dreamed about a day like this ...'

'Dreamed! That's it! Oh Clarity, darling, you've just cracked it! Clever, clever little you!'

Clarity looked at Diana in amazement.

'Pardon?'

'*A Midsummer Night's Dream*!' she cried. 'The perfect theme for the wedding. And what's more I know the very place to get your dress!'

She hurled the lavender dress at a very surprised shop assistant, grabbed Clarity's hand and dragged her through the door.

'Diana, where are we going?'

'Trust me,' cried Diana. 'Tell me, how would Henry feel about being dressed as Oberon, King of the Fairies?'

It didn't often happen but, for once in her life, Clarity Meadows was incapable of speech.

12.45 p.m.

In lunch

'Jade, I have to talk to you!' Scott elbowed his way into the queue and grabbed a plate of spaghetti. 'It's important.'

Reluctantly, Jade followed him to a table in the far corner and sat down.

'Is there something wrong?' he demanded before she had the chance to take a mouthful of food.

'I ...' she began. She couldn't say it. She couldn't say she didn't feel the same about him any more. He was looking at her wide eyed, and she knew that she had the power to make him happy or sad. She couldn't do it.

'No, everything's fine,' she said, willing herself to believe it.

'You would tell me if you were going off me, wouldn't you?' he persisted.

Jade's stomach lurched and suddenly the sight of her lunch made her feel queasy.

'Yes, you know I would,' she said.

He grinned from ear to ear and squeezed her hand.

'That's such a relief,' he said. 'You can't imagine how much better I feel.'

And you have no idea how dreadful I feel, she thought. No idea at all.

1.00 p.m.

Reckless abandon in a wine bar

'And two more glasses of Cabernet Sauvignon, please!'

Diana waved the wine list in the waiter's face.

'Diana, no!' protested Clarity, laying down her knife and fork and pushing her plate away. 'It's so expensive here and –'

'My treat!' cried Diana expansively. 'It's not every day my friend buys her wedding outfit. Aren't you pleased I took you to that theatrical outfitters?'

Clarity nodded.

'I'm just a bit worried about what Tansy will say,' she murmured. 'She's a temperamental girl at the best of times, and I'm not sure that dressing up as a fairy is quite her thing.'

'Darling, I told you, it will be fine!' cried Diana. 'Especially since you've been such a pet and decided to have Cleo as well.'

'You think she'll agree to sing?' asked Clarity. '"Love changes everything"?'

'Of course she will!' enthused Diana. 'She'll be over the moon! Everyone will be ecstatic! This is going to be a day no one will ever forget.'

2 p.m.

Red alert on the money front

'Cleo, can I have that ten pounds back?' Tansy whispered as they filed into the Science lab. 'I've got to get Mum's present after school today.'

Cleo thought fast.

'I'll bring it tomorrow,' she said. 'The thing is, I was so busy telling Mum what she had to say to your mother about the wedding and everything, that I completely forgot to ask for my allowance. I'm really sorry.'

Tansy sighed.

'OK, but be absolutely sure to bring it tomorrow, OK? promise?'

'Promise,' said Cleo.

3 p.m.

In their eighth shop since lunch

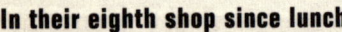

'I feel tiddly!' giggled Clarity, slipping her feet into a pair of sequinned sandals. 'You should never have made me have that extra glass of wine!'

'Red wine is good for the heart!' declared Diana 'And we want to keep your heart in good shape, don't we?'

She burst out laughing and thrust a pair of shoes at the shop assistant.

'I'll take those as well!' she cried, slapping her Visa card on to the counter.

'Diana, you've already bought three pairs!' protested Clarity. 'And they cost a fortune!'

'Oh, it's only money!' chirped Diana. 'Besides, I do so like to look good!'

The assistant leaned across the counter.

'I'm sorry, madam,' she said quietly, 'but your card has not been accepted.'

'Not accepted?' Diana coloured slightly. 'Oh, well, take this one!'

She banged an Access card down and turned to Clarity.

'Now sweetheart, let's look over there at those wonderful chiffon scarves. I think you should wrap one round your shoulders.'

She was fingering the scarves when the assistant coughed loudly.

'Madam, I'm afraid this card has been rejected as well,' she said.

Diana swallowed hard and looked at Clarity out of the corner of her eye.

'Oh well, I'll leave the shoes!' she snapped. 'There's obviously been some mistake.'

She snatched up her handbag and headed for the door.

'Diana – is everything all right?' Clarity queried. 'I mean –'

'Fine, darling, fine!' replied Diana. 'Some stupid computer error, I don't doubt.'

She bit her lip and looked away.

'Coffee?' suggested Clarity. 'I'm paying.'

'Lovely,' said Diana. 'Can I have a brandy in mine?'

3.35 p.m.

Getting ready to go home

'Cleo, what is it?'

Jade found Cleo leaning against the wall in the cloakroom, crying yet again.

'It's Scott,' mumbled Cleo.

Jade looked alarmed.

'Scott? What's wrong with him?'

'Nothing – it's just that he told me that he'd been talking to Trig on the phone, and Trig was meant to phone me and he didn't and I don't know why and do you think that means he's gone off me, but I can't see how he could because last week –'

'Hang on, hang on!' interjected Jade. 'When did Scott talk to Trig?'

'Last night,' sighed Cleo. 'I waited for ever for him to phone. Do you think he's met someone else?'

Jade frowned.

'Course not,' she said. 'Be reasonable – if he had, he would come out with it and tell you, wouldn't he? Why would he want to pretend?'

And then she stopped. Because he's scared of hurting her feelings, because he feels rotten for not loving her any more, she thought.

'I guess,' replied Cleo doubtfully. 'Jade – can you talk

to Scott? I mean, he might tell you things he wouldn't tell me. I can't bear not knowing. So will you?'

'Well, I –'

'Please!'

'OK,' sighed Jade. 'I'll see what I can do.'

4.30 p.m.

'Mum! I'm back!'

Silence. Tansy belted up the stairs and threw open her mother's bedroom door.

No one.

Clearly her mother was still shopping, which was not a good sign. If she was having second thoughts, she wouldn't be out on the town buying wedding outfits.

Sugar!

4.45 p.m.

Feeding her face

Tansy was halfway through her second cheese sandwich when an irritating ring tone made her jump.

'da-da-di-da, da-da-di-da, da-da-di-dadadadadarrrrr ...'

'When the Saints go Marching In' – that was Henry's mobile phone! She glanced round the kitchen, trying to spot it, and then realized that the sound was coming from the sitting room.

Still munching her sandwich, she followed the sound and eventually found the phone behind the battered sofa. Of course, by then it had stopped ringing.

It was, she had to admit, a dead cool phone.

It wouldn't matter if she had a little fiddle with it, just to see whether it had games or not.

It did.

Snake. The best game ever.

He wouldn't know if she had just one game.

She tucked it into her skirt pocket, stuffed the remains of the cheese sandwich into her mouth and ran upstairs.

5.15 p.m.

Aiming for the top score

' *da-da-di-da, da-da-di-da, da-da-di-dadadadadarrrrr …*'

Tansy glared at the phone as it shrilled yet again, interrupting her game.

It had rung six times in the last half hour and she was getting sick of it. There was only one thing to do.

'Hello?'

'Oh – er, I think I must have got the wrong number!' The voice was deep and really rather sexy. 'I'm sorry to have disturbed you.'

'That's OK!' said Tansy, and returned to Snake.

'*da-da-di-da, da-da-di-da, da-da-di-dadadadadarrrrr …*'

'For heaven's sake!'

She turned down the volume and ignored the call.

Minutes later, her game was interrupted by a flashing envelope sign.

Message!

Tansy eyed the phone.

Of course you should never pick up other people's messages.

But then again, it could be a matter of life and death.

And, besides, she wanted to clear the screen of the envelope.

She speed-dialled VoiceMail.

'Henry? It's me. Kyle. You have to call us. It's urgent. We don't have a clue where you are and we have to get in touch. You can't do this to us – it's been three months now! Things are so awful and it's making Mum ill ... Please, Henry. Please ring. OK? Please.'

'To listen to your message again, press one. To save your message, press two ...'

Tansy pressed number two on the keypad and leaned back in her chair.

Who was this Kyle? And what did he mean? Clearly it wasn't Henry's son – his name was Duncan.

But why would he be talking to Henry about his mum?

A nephew maybe?

But Henry kept moaning that he was an only child and so lonely.

Weird.

5.30 p.m.

'I've had a lovely day!' Cleo's mum cried as she threw carrier bags on to the table.

'Clarity's got a wonderful dress – oh, but I mustn't let on!'

She giggled slightly drunkenly.

'And now that you are going to be one of her fairy attendants and sing at the wedding –'

'I AM WHAT?'

Cleo stared at her mother open-mouthed.

'Isn't it lovely?' her mother asked, clapping her hands in delight. 'Look!'

She grabbed a carrier bag and pulled out a peach-coloured dress made of net and silver thread, a pair of tiny see-through wings and a headdress that Cleo thought resembled recycled milk-bottle tops.

'Peaseblossom!' crowed Diana. 'As in *A Midsummer Night's Dream*. And Tansy's going to be Mustardseed.'

'Tansy,' remarked Cleo through clenched teeth, 'is going to be dead by the time I've finished with her!'

5.40 p.m.

3 Plough Cottages. Going demented

'For the last time, Mum, NO!' stormed Tansy.

'But you promised!'

'I promised to be a bridesmaid,' corrected Tansy. 'Not a stupid fairy with wings. I'm not six, Mum – I'm practically fifteen!'

'Cleo's doing it,' sighed her mother.

'Cleo?' Tansy was gobsmacked. 'You are joking?'

Her mother shook her head.

'She's thrilled,' said Clarity. 'But then Cleo is the kind of girl who knows what this means to me.'

Cleo is dead meat, thought Tansy.

'And she's going to sing,' added Clarity. She fiddled with the corner of the tablecloth and looked pleadingly at Tansy.

'Please, darling. For me.'

Tansy sighed.

'There are conditions,' she said.

'Like what?'

'No wings.'

'But then no one will realize you are a fairy,' protested her mother.

'Precisely,' said Tansy. 'I rest my case.'

5.45 p.m.

In full flood

'How could you do that to me? That is so not on!'

Cleo stormed down the phone to Tansy.

'Don't shout at me!' retorted Tansy. 'I've got to do it too.'

'She's your mother!' reasoned Cleo. 'You've no choice. But to drag me into it ...'

'I didn't! I didn't know anything about it until five minutes ago. Say no if you want to.'

'I can't,' said Cleo.

'Why not?'

'It would be mean,' sighed Cleo.

'You know the trouble with us?' said Tansy.

'What?'

'We are just too nice for our own good.'

6.00 p.m.

'Is Henry is coming for supper?' asked Tansy as her mother

hurled strange shrivelled greenery into a steamer.

Her mother shook her head.

'No,' she said. 'He said he had lots to do – more secret surprises for me, I guess! He's bringing his stuff round later.' She grinned happily. 'I rather think he's arranging the honeymoon,' she said. 'Which reminds me – I asked Holly's mum to have you for half-term, OK?'

Cool, thought Tansy.

'Must I?' she said sorrowfully.

It never did to let a parent know they had made a good decision.

6.30 p.m.

A little lecture

'Mum,' said Cleo over supper, 'can I have next month's allowance now?'

'No, darling,' said Diana firmly. 'You'll have to wait till next week.'

So much, thought Cleo, for parental support!

8.00 p.m.

Oh, go away! thought Clarity irritably as the telephone rang for the third time. I'm making lists.

'Yes?'

She grabbed the receiver and dropped her pen.

'Clarity, is that you? It's Val Richards!'

Andy's mum sounded excited.

'Oh – hi!' Clarity tried to sound chirpy.

'First of all, congratulations! How exciting it all is! I'm so thrilled!'

'Thank you.'

'Andy says you would like me to make the cake?'

'Well, if you don't mind ...'

'Mind? I'd adore it! This is such fun!'

That was a change, Clarity thought. Someone who actually took pleasure in her happiness.

'Now, Clarity, this is a silly question really, but with you being a gardener and everything, I was wondering ...'

'You want some work done?' Clarity sounded hopeful. She'd been rather extravagant lately and some extra gardening work would be very welcome.

'Oh no!' laughed Val. 'Can't afford that. No, I was wondering about names.'

'Names?'

'For the twins,' explained Val. 'You see, when Andy got together with Tansy, I just fell in love with her name and I want plant names for the babies. Well, it's easy for girls, isn't it? I mean, I thought Saffron or Poppy or perhaps Daisy or even Clover ...'

'Lovely,' murmured Clarity, wondering what on earth all this had to do with her.

'But then, if one of them is a boy....well, you can't call a kid Parsley or Chickweed, can you?' she giggled. 'And with you being a horticultural sort of person ...'

'Right,' agreed Clarity. 'Well, I'll give it some thought. And by the way, you will come on Saturday, won't you?'

'Saturday?'

'The wedding. Noon. In the castle ruins and then

afterwards ... oh golly, I haven't thought about afterwards! Oh no!'

'Off to the pub?' suggested Val.

'I'll let you know,' said Clarity. 'Oh crumbs!'

8.20 p.m.

Tansy was still struggling to write her English essay in between games of Snake, when Henry's phone rang again.

Without thinking, she pressed OK.

'Hello?'

'Look, is that 07970 634497?'

'I don't know,' began Tansy.

'What do you mean, you don't know?'

'It's not my phone,' she explained.

'Oh, so you go around picking up other people's phones, do you?' The boy on the other end sounded exasperated.

'No – I mean, it's Henry's phone and –'

'Oh. So it ... ight ... ber!'

Tansy frowned and moved towards the window. The phone signal was breaking up.

'Sorry,' she said. 'Bad signal. What was that?'

'So put ... ry ... ine now!'

Click.

The signal had died.

But almost immediately, the phone rang again.

'Hello!' Tansy snapped.

'Tansy? Henry here. So you've found my phone!'

'Yes.'

'Thank God for that!' He sounded relieved. 'I don't suppose anyone has rung?'

Tansy hesitated. If she admitted they had, he'd be mad at her for answering his calls, and besides, she'd noticed that the battery was failing after all her attempts at Snake.

'Don't know,' she lied. 'Oh yes – it says there's a message waiting.'

'OK, fine, well just put the phone somewhere safe, OK? And leave it alone!'

He sounded flustered.

'I'm expecting an important message from an ex-colleague,' he went on. 'I don't want anyone fiddling with the phone and deleting it, OK? Oh, and tell your mother I'll be over in an hour – Bye!'

Tansy put the phone to one side and then picked it up again.

She pressed number one on the keypad and listened to the message again.

'Henry? It's me. Kyle. You have to call us. It's urgent. We don't have a clue where you are and we have to get in touch. You can't do this to us – it's been three months now! Things are so awful and it's making Mum ill. Please, Henry. Please ring. OK? Please.'

Tansy frowned.

It's been three months now!

Her mum met Henry about three months ago.

Something very odd was going on.

Two minutes later

She had pressed number two on the keypad and saved the message.

A saved message meant someone had already read it.

Henry would go ape.

Three minutes later

I am without doubt a rather brilliant person, thought Tansy, punching Holly's phone number into Henry's phone.

'Hello?'

'Holly, it's me, Tansy. Listen, ring me back on this number now – only I won't answer. You have to leave a message, only don't speak – just mumble, or groan or something. OK?'

'Tansy?' said Holly

'What?'

'Have you been drinking?'

'Just do it, Holly. Just do a 1471 to get the number, write it down, save it and then phone it. And mumble, OK? I'll explain later. Oh, and when you've done it, ring me back on our land line, OK?'

Five minutes later

'Brilliant!' Tansy grinned at the sound of Holly's voice. 'Did you leave a really indistinct message?'

'You bet!' laughed Holly. 'I stuffed my mouth full of Mars bar and spoke through a tea towel – in French!'

Tansy giggled.

'Ace!'

'Now,' said Holly, 'would you mind telling me what is going on?'

'It's a long story,' said Tansy.

'Good,' said Holly. 'Anything to put off writing that essay.'

Ten minutes later

'So now,' concluded Tansy, 'he'll see that there is a message waiting and won't know that I listened to the first one.'

'Which you've now deleted,' added Holly.

'Had to,' agreed Tansy, 'otherwise the voicemail would have told him there was a saved message as well. Get it?'

'Mmm,' murmured Holly. 'So who is this Kyle?'

'How should I know?' retorted Tansy. 'But I've got a feeling that there's something a bit dodgy going on. The guy sounded pretty desperate.'

'So where was he phoning from?'

'I don't know.'

'You mean, you didn't scroll to *Last Calls Received*? What are you on?'

Tansy gasped.

'That's an idea!' she cried. 'Hang on – give me two minutes and I'll call you back!'

Fifteen minutes later

'Tansy! Henry's here – where did you put his phone?'

Oh flip and fried sausages! thought Tansy, scribbling down the number and stuffing the piece of paper into her shoe.

'Coming!' she called.

THURSDAY

8.00 a.m.

Tansy clattered downstairs and stopped dead. The sitting room was packed with cardboard boxes, suit carriers, and a music system with speakers the size of small bungalows. There was hardly a centimetre of floor space left uncovered.

Henry was clearly not short of possessions.

Tansy was edging her way past the boxes when the phone rang.

She grabbed the receiver.

'Hello?'

'Is that Clarity Meadows?'

Tansy didn't recognize the voice on the other end.

'No, it's Tansy, her daughter, but I'll –'

'Daughter? Good grief, I didn't know there was a daughter.'

'Pardon?'

'My father. I didn't realize he was taking on a kid as well.'

'I'm not a kid, I'm nearly fifteen and anyway, he ...' She stopped as the full impact of the woman's words hit her.

'Henry's your father? Are you Deborah?'

'Yes,' replied the woman shortly. 'Is he there? I'm calling from Melbourne.'

'I'll get him.'

Tansy left the receiver swinging and went to the kitchen door.

'Henry? Phone! You daughter!'

She stuck her head round the door.

'Deborah?' Henry looked up in surprise. 'On the phone?'

'Yes – from Australia!'

Henry stood up and hesitated. Then he hurried to the phone, shutting the kitchen door firmly behind him.

'Isn't that lovely?' sighed Clarity. 'Deborah must be phoning up to congratulate us – Henry e-mailed her yesterday.'

She gestured to the corner of the kitchen where a laptop sat on top of the counter.

'He says that he'll get me a Psion organizer when ...'

But Tansy wasn't listening. She was straining to catch Henry's words.

'Don't be silly ... what? What do you mean – Kyle? He hasn't ... No, Deborah, don't you dare tell her! Deborah? I won't let you ... Deb? Damn!'

The phone was slammed down.

'Was she thrilled, darling?' Clarity beamed up at him as he came back into the kitchen.

'Over the moon! On top of the world! Just devastated that she can't be here.'

Henry's lips formed a smile but his eyes were darting anxiously from left to right.

'Look,' he said, 'I must dash – just remembered some bits and pieces still left to do.'

'But Henry,' gasped Clarity, 'we were going to sort out the reception and –'

'You do it, my poppet,' he gabbled. 'I know you'll cope beautifully. See you later.'

And with that, he snatched up his jacket and was gone.

10.15 a.m.

Brainstorming the situation

'There's definitely something dodgy about him,' Tansy said to Holly for the tenth time that morning. 'First that Kyle guy and his weird message, and now Henry arguing with his daughter and mentioning Kyle's name.'

'Did you tell your mum what you overheard?'

'No,' admitted Tansy. 'She was getting all flustered over wedding cakes and bouquets. I didn't have the heart.'

'You,' sighed Holly, 'are getting very soft.'

Noon. Question time

'Scott, I need to ask you something.'

Jade grabbed his arm as they left the Science lab.

'What?'

'You know you talk to Trig on the phone,' Jade began, 'well, does he ever mention Cleo?'

'Sometimes,' he mumbled. 'Why?'

'So, he says he's missing her and everything?'

'I didn't say that,' Scott corrected her.

'What do you mean?'

Scott hesitated.

'Well,' he murmured. 'Actually, what he says is that he wishes she'd leave him alone and stop coming on strong all the time.'

Jade's mouth dropped open.

'He's got a new girlfriend,' Scott went on. 'He's crazy about her. And Cleo keeps calling him and he's getting really stroppy about it.'

Jade sighed.

'So why doesn't he have the decency to tell Cleo?'

Scott shrugged.

'I guess he hasn't got the guts,' said Scott.

'That's so hypocritical …' began Jade. And stopped.

She was doing just the same thing to Scott. Pretending to be in love when she wasn't. Letting him think things were hunky-dory instead of coming clean.

She'd have to tell him the truth.

It was only fair.

She'd do it.

Another day.

12.15 p.m.

Standing her ground

'Will you tell Cleo?' Scott asked Jade as they walked to the cafeteria. 'I mean, Trig asked me to, but you're her friend and besides, she'd probably cry and then I wouldn't know what to do and –'

'No,' said Jade firmly. 'Tell Trig to phone her and do it himself.'

'I probably won't be talking to him for ages,' admitted Scott. 'He's a bit miffed with me.'

'Why?'

'He invited me to go and stay with him for Christmas and New Year and I said no.'

Jade gasped.

'You said NO? Why on earth would you do that?' She hesitated. 'Oh – is it the air fare? I mean, I know it costs a lot and ...'

Scott shook his head.

'No,' he said. 'Trig's parents are offering to pay. It's you.'

'Me?'

Jade stared at him.

'I couldn't leave you over Christmas,' Scott said. 'It wouldn't be fair. Besides, I couldn't enjoy anything without you.'

He squeezed her hand.

'So don't worry. I'm not going. I'm staying here right beside you.'

Jade knew she should say something.

But what? How?

Why was life so complicated?

1.15 p.m.

In the locker room. Seeking advice

'Legs? Can I have a word?'

Jade caught up with her cousin as the bell for afternoon lessons rang.

'Sure – what is it?'

'When Hugo dumped you –'

'He didn't dump me, we came to a mutual arrangement!' snapped Allegra.

Jade looked at her quizzically.

'OK, so he dumped me,' agreed Allegra with a sigh. 'What about it?'

'How did he tell you?'

'He said that he didn't think that we had anything in common any more,' she snarled. 'Why?'

Jade eyed her.

'I need to tell Scott it's over, but I don't know how,' she sighed.

'Just tell him straight,' said Allegra eagerly. 'Is it really over?'

Jade nodded.

'Wow!' gasped Allegra.

2.15 p.m.

Seeking more advice

'Holly?' asked Jade. 'How exactly did Paul tell you that he just wanted to be friends?'

Holly frowned.

'He said he didn't want to get serious with anyone,' she sighed. 'Why?'

'Me and Scott ...' began Jade.

'You're not planning to chuck him, are you?' gasped Holly.

Jade nodded.

'He'll be devastated!' exclaimed Holly.

'Tell me about it,' sighed Jade. 'But the thing is, Trig's invited him to the States and Scott won't go because he doesn't want to leave me.'

'That,' said Holly, 'is true love.'

'That,' said Jade, 'is stupidity.'

'You,' said Holly, 'are not a romantic.'

'That,' agreed Jade, 'is very true.'

4.00 p.m.

Maternal intervention

'Door's open!' yelled Tansy's mum as the front door bell shrilled.

It shrilled again.

Clarity sighed, straightened from emptying boxes in the sitting room and opened the front door.

'MUM!'

Standing on the doorstep wearing a scarlet fur hat and a very sour expression was Tansy's grandmother.

'Right,' said her mother, marching straight into the house. 'What's going on? Honestly, I turn my back for five minutes and you go and get yourself into another mess.'

Clarity refrained from reminding her mother that it had been two and a half years since they had seen one another.

'So what's all this about marriage? And where did you find this Henry? These sofas are a disgrace; can't you get them re-covered? And what's that vase doing over there?

It's quite the wrong colour for this room.'

Clarity bit her lip and began counting to ten.

'Tea, Mum?' she sighed.

'Earl Grey,' ordered her mother. 'No sugar, a splash of milk. And then I want to talk to you, young lady.'

4.45 p.m.

'Hi, Mum!' Tansy crashed into the kitchen. 'Oh. Gran. Hi.' Tansy swallowed hard.

'Your hair needs cutting,' commented her grandmother. 'Come and kiss me.'

Tansy pecked her cheek.

'Well, I've had a word with your mother and, as usual, she won't take a blind bit of notice. Says she loves this Henry.'

She spoke as if Clarity was suddenly invisible.

'I told you she was out of control. Always has been.'

6.15 p.m.

Henry meets his match

'Henry darling!' Clarity looked rather nervous as her fiancé burst into the sitting room. 'This is my mother – Mum, this is Henry!'

Tansy's grandmother eased herself out of her armchair and surveyed Henry critically from head to toe.

'Good God!' she said. 'Well, your dress sense is as bizarre as my daughter's, but at least she's attractive.'

'Mum!' Clarity gasped, as Tansy tried desperately not to laugh.

'You're far too old for Clarity,' her gran went on. 'You'd do better to marry me – not that I'd have you!'

Henry laughed nervously.

'My little flower petal and I will be just fine,' he assured her. 'Won't we, pumpkin pie?'

'Don't be ridiculous!' snorted Tansy's gran.

Suddenly, Tansy had a great desire to hug her to bits.

10.15 p.m.

Answer it, Trig. Please, please answer it.

'You have reached the voicemail of Trig Roscoe. Please leave a message ...'

'TRIG! Trig, I love you. Please phone me. Please. Please.'

Cleo put down the phone and burst into tears.

Why didn't he call? If he was going off her, she would die.

She knew she would.

8.00 a.m.

Striking a deal

'Portia, can I borrow ten pounds?'

'No way!'

'Please – it's really urgent. If I don't pay Tansy back, she'll never speak to me again. Please.'

'On one condition,' said Portia.

'What?'

'You do all my chores for two weeks.'

'That is so not on!'

'Suit yourself!' smirked Portia.

'One week,' declared Cleo firmly.

'Ten days!'

'Done.'

8.45 a.m

School. Again. TGIF

'You look dreadful,' Holly said to Tansy as they jostled their way up the stairs to the classroom.

'So would you if your mother was going to marry a moron in just over twenty-four hours,' sighed Tansy.

Holly nodded.

'It occurs to me,' she mused ,'that you ought to phone that guy.'

'What guy?' queried Tansy.

'The one that left the messages on the answerphone,' explained Holly. 'I mean, if there is something dodgy, we ought to know about it.'

8.50 a.m.

In the classroom. Thinking

'You're right!' exclaimed Tansy.

'I usually am,' smiled Holly. 'What about this time?'

'I'm going to phone Kyle,' Tansy said. 'I've got his number in my purse. I'll phone him at break.'

9 a.m.

'I've come for breakfast, much good may it do me!'

Tansy's grandmother stood in the doorway, frowning

at her daughter.

'Where's Henry?'

'In the bath,' said Clarity.

'You mean – he slept here?'

Clarity nodded.

'Huh!' Her mother sniffed. 'There are things about the modern age I don't care for! Beth wouldn't behave like that ...'

'Oh well, of course she wouldn't!' shouted Clarity. 'Beth always was your favourite. She could do no wrong and I could do no right!' She banged her fist on the table. 'Well, if you can't be nice to me, go home!' she shouted. 'I'm sick of everyone getting at me.'

To her amazement, her mother said nothing. She just sank into a chair and put her head in her hands.

And Clarity saw that her shoulders were shaking.

Her mother never cried. Her mother had no emotion.

Clarity didn't know what to do.

9.25 a.m.

Building bridges

'I didn't mean to shout,' said Clarity, passing her mother a tissue.

'Yes you did,' replied her mother. 'And rightly so.'

She sighed and gazed at Clarity.

'Oh Clarity, I made such a mess of bringing you up,' she said. 'But I never meant to get it all wrong.'

'What do you mean?' asked Clarity, still fazed by her mother's sudden softening.

'What I mean,' explained her mother, 'is that I was too demanding, too strict, too determined to make you a clone of me and too – oh, unmotherly, I guess.'

Clarity was about to deny it all, and stopped. It was true. Her mother had been overbearing and harsh. She had always wanted her own way. Clarity said nothing.

'So when Beth came along – and that was a surprise, I can tell you! – I decided to get it right that time,' she said. 'I read all the childcare books and went to parenting classes, and I tried to be laid back. And I guess I got a bit better at it, and she was more – well, friendly.'

Clarity nodded slowly.

'You were a very difficult child,' sighed her mother.

'You were a pretty awkward mother,' said Clarity. 'You're still so angry with me all the time. I mean, I know I ran away and got pregnant and –'

'No, I'm not angry with you, I'm angry with me,' admitted her mother. 'I adored you, Clarity. And I guess I wanted you to be perfect.' She sighed. 'But perfect isn't possible, is it? I love you. I just never knew how to tell you.'

10.30 a.m.

'Here's your money,' said Cleo, thrusting ten pounds at Tansy. 'What are you getting your mum?'

'A photo frame and then I'm putting in loads of pictures of her and me,' said Tansy. 'Do you think that's naff?'

'I think it's lovely,' smiled Cleo. 'And I assume there won't be any of Henry?'

'You assume right,' Tansy assured her.

10.45 a.m.

'Have you told him yet?' Allegra rushed up to Jade, Holly and Cleo in the schoolyard.

'Told who what?' asked Jade.

'Scott!' stressed Allegra in exasperation. 'Have you told him it's over?'

'Over?' Cleo gasped. 'Jade, you can't! You can't do that to him!'

'Why can't she?' demanded Holly.

'It's my life!' interjected Jade.

'Too right,' agreed Holly. 'You're a free woman, aren't you? Like me,' she added with a sigh.

10.55 a.m.

'Have you done it?' Holly demanded as Tansy came out of the locker room. 'Have you phoned Kyle?'

Tansy shook her head.

'I don't dare,' she admitted

'Oh please!' Holly sighed. 'Do you want to know the whole truth about Henry, yes or no?'

'Yes.'

'And are you likely to find it out by being a total wimp? Yes or no?'

'No.'

'So,' said Holly. 'Do it.'

Three minutes later

'Is that Kyle? Oh, hi. This is Tansy Meadows speaking. We talked when you phoned Henry Fazackerley, and I wondered whether he'd called you back OK?'

She covered the mouthpiece and turned to Holly.

'He didn't.'

'Curiouser and curiouser,' muttered Holly.

Tansy winced as a torrent of angry words burst from the phone.

'He never does? ... He's a what? ... Oh, a slime ball. I know.'

She gave Holly the thumbs-up sign.

'What? ... A crooked what? ... Really?'

She mouthed at Holly.

'We're not allowed to use words like that!'

She turned her attention back to the phone.

'What? ... Of course I know where he is ... The address?'

She looked at Holly.

'He wants the address,' she hissed. 'He says he has a bone to pick with Henry.'

'Oh goody,' grinned Holly. 'So tell him. This sounds like it might be just what we need.'

1 p.m.

Picking at a tuna salad. Bathed in guilt

'I shouldn't have done it,' moaned Tansy. 'It's all your fault. I should never have listened to you.'

'Oh nonsense!' declared Holly. 'If this Kyle really does

have dirt to dish on Henry, then we should know about it. If he doesn't, then there's no harm done, is there?'

Tansy sighed deeply and said nothing.

'Don't worry,' said Holly. 'By the way, if you're not going to eat that salad, can I have it?'

2 p.m.

'The cake is divine!' Clarity stood in Val Richards' kitchen and clapped her hands in glee. 'You are clever!'

She sank down on a chair and sighed deeply.

'What's wrong?' asked Val. 'Is it the icing? I did wonder about the colour but –'

'No, no it's perfect!' Clarity assured her. 'It's Tansy.'

'Tansy?'

'She doesn't seem to get on with Henry. And I just so want everything to be perfect.'

Val patted her shoulder.

'Don't worry,' she said. 'Kids take time to accept change. Andy was furious about these babies –' she patted her huge stomach lovingly – 'and now he can't wait for them to be born!'

Well, she thought, a little white lie can't hurt.

'You mark my words,' she continued, 'it will all ... aaaahhh!'

She grabbed the corner of the table and winced in pain.

'What is it?' gasped Clarity. 'Are you OK?'

'Ooooooh!' Val exhaled loudly. 'Sorry, just a twinge!' she said

'The babies! It's not –'

'No, silly,' grinned Val, sinking down into a chair. 'They're not due for two months. It's just wind. I get it a lot these days. I'm fine now.'

'Thank goodness for that!' breathed Clarity. 'I can't do with any more crises right now.'

2.30 p.m.

'I'll see you tomorrow, darling!' Clarity wrapped her arms around Henry. 'Are you sure you don't mind staying in the hotel tonight?'

'Of course not!' Henry cried. 'After all, I mustn't see the bride until the big moment, must I?'

Clarity gave him a wave and went back into the kitchen.

'Henry, wait!' Clarity rushed back outside. 'You've forgotten your phone again.'

'No, darling, you can chuck that one! Got a new one!'

He fished a bright red phone from his pocket and waved it in her face.

'Oh – and a new number!' he cried. '07970 ...'

'Wait! I'll get a pen!'

Clarity dashed back into the house as Henry slipped his new phone back into his pocket.

'And now he can ring me for all he's worth,' he murmured to himself. 'He can ring till he's blue in the face.'

5 p.m.

The things we do for mothers

This, thought Tansy, is like something out of a nightmare.

She and Cleo were standing in the sitting room dressed as fairies.

'You look lovely!' cried Clarity, clapping her hands. 'Don't they, Diana?'

'Cherubic,' agreed Diana. 'Although they really should be wearing the wings.'

'No wings!' cried Cleo and Tansy in unison.

'Pink chiffon with tinsel and sequins is bad enough,' said Tansy.

'And as for these wands ...' added Cleo. 'I feel like something out of a third-rate pantomime.'

'Oh stop complaining!' cried Diana. 'Now what about showing them your outfit, Clarity?'

'I'm keeping it a secret,' said Clarity. 'They'll only laugh.'

7 p.m.

Shocks over supper

'You're not eating, Mum,' said Tansy.

'I'm too on edge to eat,' replied her mother.

'You've got to eat,' ordered Tansy's grandmother. 'You'll only get silly if you get low blood sugar.'

'Don't boss, Mum. I'm a grown woman.'

'Sorry,' said Tansy's gran.

Both Tansy and her mother were so stunned to hear an apology from the woman who was never in the wrong, that neither of them swallowed another mouthful for at least five minutes.

7.30 p.m.

Fit or what?

'Who's that?' demanded Tansy's gran as the front-door bell rang.

'I don't know, I left my crystal ball upstairs,' said Tansy sweetly.

'Don't be cheeky,' said her gran. But she was grinning.

Tansy opened the door. Standing on the step, wearing a suede jacket to die for, was the fittest guy she had seen in a long time. He looked about nineteen and towered over her, and when he spoke his voice sent little shivers down her spine.

'I'm Kyle Woodward,' he said, holding out a bronzed hand. 'Sorry – I thought this would be an office address. I'm looking for –'

'Henry Fazackerley,' said Tansy. 'I know. It was me you spoke to.'

'You?' Kyle looked astonished. 'I didn't realize you were so young.'

Tansy glowered.

'Anyway, I got here as fast as I could. Can I come in?'

'Sure.' She waved him into the sitting room, wishing that she wasn't wearing her most ancient pair of jeans and that her grandmother wasn't sitting in the armchair eating pear drops.

'Henry's not here,' Tansy began. 'He's gone to The White Horse for the night because of the wedding –'

'Wedding?' Kyle looked taken aback.

'Yes. He and my mother are getting married tomorrow.'

'Good God!'

Kyle's hand flew to his mouth and he eyed Tansy in horror.

'He can't! I mean, they can't! How can he do that to my mum?'

Tansy's brain went on red alert.

'Your mum?'

'Don't tell me,' interjected her grandmother, rising with difficulty from her armchair and peering at him, 'that Henry is your father too?'

Kyle looked horrified.

'No, he most certainly is not!' he exploded. 'Thank God!'

'I think,' said Tansy's grandmother, 'that you had better sit down. And begin at the beginning.'

8 p.m.

More shocks for Clarity

'Tra la la, it's my happy happy day! Tra la la ... oh!'

Tansy's mother stopped halfway down the stairs and gasped.

Tansy and her grandmother looked up at her, their faces pale and expressionless.

'I didn't realize we had a visitor,' she began. 'Who's this? What's going on?'

Tansy swallowed.

'Mum, this is Kyle. Kyle Woodward. He ... he knows Henry.'

'Oh lovely! Someone to be on Henry's side for the wedding. I was feeling really bad –'

'I'll never be on Henry's side!' Kyle took two steps across the room. 'After what he's done to my mother, I'll never trust that man again!'

8.15 p.m.

The truth comes out

Clairty sank down on to the bottom stair and gripped the banister.

'I think,' said Tansy's grandmother, 'that you should hear what this young man has to say. Go on, Kyle. Tell her.'

'My mum met Henry last year,' said Kyle flatly. 'She fell madly in love with him, heaven knows why …'

'Love?' Clarity gasped.

'… And he moved in.'

'He seems to do a lot of that,' murmured Tansy's grandmother.

'They set a date for the wedding, he bought her a ring and everything …' Kyle went on.

'What?' There was a strangled gasp from Clarity.

'Henry said he would set Mum up in her own market garden once they were married,' said Kyle. 'She'd done a lot of gardening and landscaping, set up a thriving business from home …'

Clarity let out a little cry.

'… And she was making a fair bit of money, but she wanted to expand. Henry was some sort of plant expert, or so he said, and he persuaded Mum to open a joint bank account so that he could put money in. Only he didn't.'

'What?' gasped Tansy.

'Six months later, he was gone,' said Kyle. 'With ten thousand pounds of Mum's hard-earned cash.'

'Oh my God!' Clarity swayed and grabbed the back of a chair.

Kyle stared at her hand.

'What's that?' His voice was strained. 'That ring – it's the one he gave my mum. He said it was an antique, a family heirloom. It was the only decent thing he ever gave her. And now –' his voice cracked – 'he's given it to you.'

As if in slow motion, Clarity's head dropped, she put her face in her hands and began to sob.

8.30 p.m.

Mopping up mother

'Mum, don't cry,' begged Tansy, handing her mother another cup of tea and putting an arm round her shoulders. 'Just think what a lucky escape you've had.'

'But I love him,' sobbed Clarity.

'No,' said Tansy's gran gently. 'You love the man you thought he was.'

Clarity raised a tear-stained face and sighed.

'How did you know where to find us – and him – Kyle?' she asked.

Tansy threw him a beseeching glance and shook her head.

'I rang his mobile phone and when your daughter answered, I pretended to be checking details for the phone account,' he said, giving Tansy a faint smile. 'She had no idea she was giving the address to anyone other than the telecom people.'

Tansy threw him a grateful glance.

'I think,' said Clarity, her face crumpling again, 'that if you don't mind, I'm going up to my room. I'd like to be alone for a while.'

She paused halfway up the stairs.

'Kyle, will you do me a favour? Don't speak to Henry until tomorrow. Please.'

'Why? I just want to get my hands on him ...'

'Please,' repeated Tansy's mother. 'You've waited long enough. A few more hours won't hurt.'

'But I've got to get home ...' he began.

'Stay here,' ordered Clarity. 'We've got sleeping bags and the sofa is comfortable enough. Please.'

He nodded, looking bewildered.

'OK,' he said. 'But tomorrow I intend to confront Henry, whatever you say.'

Clarity turned away, her shoulders shaking again.

'I'll phone Mrs Vine,' offered Tansy, 'and tell her that tomorrow is cancelled.'

'You will do no such thing!' Clarity's voice was strident and determined. 'Nothing is cancelled, do you understand me? Nothing at all.'

'But, Mum ...'

'But, Clarity dearest ...'

Tansy and her gran spoke as one.

'You can't go ahead with this wedding,' gasped Tansy. 'Not now. Not knowing what you know.'

'It's total insanity!' gasped her grandmother. 'You can't do it!'

Clarity took a deep breath and tossed her head.
'Oh, can't I?' she said. 'Just you watch me.'

9.45 p.m.

'Mum! Mum! let me in, please.'

Tansy banged on her mother's locked bedroom door.

'I'm going to sleep!' Clarity's voice was muffled but steady. 'I've got a big day tomorrow. And you should be in bed too!'

'But, Mum ...'

'Goodnight, Tansy.'

'Night, Mum.'

There was no doubt about it, she thought miserably as she undressed, children should have the right to get their parents certified.

saturday

7.15 a.m.

Having a quiet word

'Angela? Clarity here. I need to have a word with you but you have to promise faithfully not to mention a word of this to anyone else. There's been a bit of an upset ...'

7.30 a.m.

Having another quiet word

'Cleo? Tansy's mum here. Look, I'm sorry to ring so early but it's about your song for the wedding ... Yes, yes, of course I still want you to sing. It's just that, well, is it too late to change the song? I know you can do it – I heard you sing it at the school concert. What I'd like is this ...'

7.45 a.m.

Further subterfuge

'Diana? Clarity ... What? ... Excited? Sort of.'

She swallowed hard and willed herself not to cry.

'Now listen, about Henry's costume for the wedding ... yes, I know it's at the hotel. But what I'd like you to do is this ...'

8 a.m.

And the final stroke!

'Kyle!' Clarity hissed down the stairs to where Kyle was rolling up his sleeping bag. 'Can I have a word?'

'Of course,' he said. 'Can I do something to help?'

'You most certainly can,' declared Clarity. 'Now listen carefully. This is what I want you to do.'

8.05 a.m.

Having the last word

'Good morning!' Clarity tightened the belt on her housecoat and held her head high. 'Ready for the fun?'

'Fun?' Tansy said. 'Mum, you can't do this ...'

'Tansy, trust me,' begged her mother. 'That's all I ask. Just for a bit longer. Trust me.'

'OK,' sighed Tansy. 'But I think you're mad.'

8.30 a.m.

'She's doing it,' said Tansy to Holly, gripping the phone with both hands.

'She's WHAT?'

'She's marrying him,' sobbed Tansy. 'And there's nothing we can do to stop her.'

8.45 a.m.

'Mum, that's enough!' Clarity turned to face her mother. 'I know what I'm doing. I'd like you to be there, but if you don't want to ...'

'How can I be there and watch you marry a hardened con man? Watch you throw your life away?' demanded her mother.

'Please come,' said Tansy softly.

'Please,' added Clarity.

Tansy's gran sighed.

'Of course I'll come,' she said taking both their hands. 'But don't expect me to be happy about it.'

10.30 a.m.

Fashion facts

'Tansy? It's Andy. Can you settle an argument?'

Tansy sighed. She didn't think she could stand any more trauma.

'It's my mother,' said Andy in tones of disgust. 'She says I have to wear a tie to the wedding. I don't, do I?'

'Andy,' replied Tansy. 'When you see what I have been ordered to wear, you will consider a tie a lucky escape.'

10.45 a.m.

'Tansy? It's Jade. I need some advice.'

  'Not you too?'

  'Pardon?'

  'Nothing.'

  'Anyway, can you ask your mum if I can bring Scott to the wedding? He's miffed because he can't spend the day with me and I thought –'

  'You said you were dumping him,' commented Tansy.

  'Well, I am but that's next week and –'

  'So if you invite him to a wedding you're sending out mixed messages,' said Tansy. 'Not that I care. Do what you like. Everyone else is.'

11.10 a.m.

'I feel an idiot,' sighed Cleo, pirouetting in her fairy costume.

  'Me too,' agreed Tansy. 'At least you don't have to let your boyfriend see you looking this.'

  To her horror, Cleo burst into tears.

  'Oh Cleo, I'm sorry – I didn't mean to mention ...'

'It's OK!' Cleo smeared a hand over her eyes. 'It's just that I know he's gone off me. Any day now he's going to phone and say it's over. I know he is.'

'No, he won't,' murmured Tansy soothingly.

'What do you know?'

Too much, thought Tansy. And then again, not enough.

11.25 a.m.

'Oh, Mum!' Tansy breathed. 'You look beautiful!'

'Darling!' Tansy's grandmother had tears in her eyes. 'That is exquisite.'

'Wow!' Cleo was speechless.

Clarity stood halfway down the stairs dressed in a floaty peach-coloured silk dress over which were layers and layers of fine lace. Wound through her diamante tiara were tiny peach rosebuds.

'I wanted a dream wedding,' she said with a catch in her voice, 'but somehow it's turning into something of a nightmare.'

'You can still cancel!' Tansy and her gran cried in unison. 'Stay at home!'

'Oh no!' Clarity's chin jutted out defiantly. 'No way. No way at all.'

12.10 p.m.

'How many more times do we have to drive round and round?' demanded Tansy, who was squashed into the back of the taxi with Cleo and her grandmother.

'It's traditional for the bride to be late,' remarked her grandmother. 'But I think one can overdo it.'

'Right!' Clarity said firmly. 'Let's go. Let's get on with it.'

12.11 p.m.

'What IS Henry wearing?' Tansy stared as she clambered out of the car and straightened her dress.

'He's Oberon,' remarked her mother, smoothing her dress. 'King of the Fairies.'

Henry was dressed in gold breeches with a gold and orange beaded waistcoat and a long velvet cape.

'Huh!' said Tansy's grandmother. 'He looks like an overripe mango.'

'Why is he dancing about like that?' asked Cleo.

'I wonder,' mused Clarity smugly.

It occurred to Tansy that her mum knew something she didn't.

Henry dashed over to them, the bells on his patent boots jangling.

'I thought you weren't coming,' cried Henry. 'I thought you'd changed your mind.'

'Darling!' Clarity flung her arms round his neck. 'Why on earth would I do a thing like that?'

Henry kissed her briefly and then began scratching his neck frantically.

'Something wrong, Henry?' asked Clarity sweetly.

'What? Oh, er – no, no. Everything's fine.'

'In your dreams,' murmured Clarity under her breath. 'In your dreams.'

12.12 p.m.

Murmuring sweet nothings

'One day we'll be doing this, won't we?' smiled Scott.

'What?' asked Jade.

'Getting married,' he said shyly.

Jade's heart sank. She couldn't put it off any longer. She would have to tell him.

Just as soon as the wedding was over.

12.20 p.m.

'Now, if we could just get on with things ...' The registrar glanced at her watch. 'Who is giving you away?'

'Me,' said Clarity.

'Oh,' said the registrar. 'Then let's begin.'

Tansy and Cleo took their places behind Clarity and everyone gathered round the few fallen stones in the centre of what had once been the castle keep.

'Ladies and gentlemen, we are gathered here ...' began the registrar.

'Not yet!' said Clarity. 'Cleo has to sing first.'

The registrar glanced at her watch, tapped her foot and sighed.

'Very well,' she muttered.

Cleo moved forward and began to sing.

'That's not the song,' hissed Tansy to her mother.

'Oh, yes it is,' muttered Clarity over her shoulder.

'Don't think, oh no, don't think you can cheat on me,

don't you think, don't you think, you can do me down ...'

Tansy caught sight of the puzzled expressions on the guests' faces as slowly, she and her mother walked to the centre of the castle keep and Clarity took her place beside Henry, who was surreptitiously scratching his right shoulder.

'I'm not some silly fool that you can play around with – oh oh NOOOOOO!'

Cleo hit the high note and looked nervously at Clarity and Henry.

'Ladies and gentlemen,' began the registrar, 'we are gathered here today ...'

'Aaaaah!!'

Everyone gasped and turned to see who had screamed. It was Andy's mum.

She was doubled up, clutching her stomach and staring at Henry.

'Hen ... aaaaaah!!!'

Henry stared back, paled and took a step backwards.

'I'm so sorry – I don't know what ... Henry!' gasped Andy's mum. 'Aaaaaah!'

'Mum!' Andy cried and rushed to her side. 'What is it?'

His mother sank to her knees on the grass.

'Ooooh – no, no!' She panted for breath. 'Henry –you brute ... how could you? Oh – the pain!!'

Tansy hurled her wand on the ground and ran over to Val, followed by Clarity.

'Andy, your mum's dress – it's all wet!' gasped Tansy

'My waters – they've broken!' gasped Andy's mum. 'It's the babies – they're coming. And I think they're coming very quickly.'

'I'll get help!' shrieked Andy. 'Phone, someone!'

His mum rolled over on to her side and winced in pain. Tansy's mum dropped down on her knees beside her.

'Clarity,' whispered Val, seizing Clarity's hand. 'Don't do it! Don't marry that man! He ... aaagh!!!'

'Don't worry,' murmured Clarity. 'Everything's going to be just fine.'

12.30 p.m.

'Excuse me,' said the registrar to the paramedics, 'but could you move that ambulance? I have a wedding to conduct.'

'Sorry, love,' said the senior paramedic. 'Can't do that. Not right now.'

'And why not?' asked the registrar.

From within the ambulance came the unmistakable wail of a new-born baby.

'That,' grinned the paramedic, 'is why not.'

Two minutes later

'We need to get these two to hospital – and fast!' said the ambulance man. 'They are premature and rather tiny.'

'I'm coming too!' cried Andy, clambering into the ambulance. 'They will – she will – be all right?' His voice faltered.

'The quicker we get there, the better they will all be,' declared the paramedic. 'Let's go!'

'What did she have?' called Clarity.

'A girl and a boy,' the man replied.

'Tell her Clover and Basil,' called Clarity. 'You will tell her, won't you?'

The man nodded and shut the rear doors of the ambulance.

'Basil? Basil?' repeated Tansy, turning to her mum.

'What on earth ...?

'It's a herb,' said Clarity calmly. 'She wanted plants.'

Tansy looked at Cleo and shrugged.

'Beyond help,' she sighed. 'Totally beyond help.'

12.55 p.m.

Nuptials begin

'Henry, do you take Clarity to be your lawful wedded wife?'

The registrar was rushing through the words as if she had a train to catch.

'I do,' smiled Henry, scratching his left thigh.

The registrar turned to Clarity.

'And, Clarity, do you take Henry to be your lawful wedded husband?'

Silence.

The registrar nodded at Clarity.

And then gave her a glare.

'Do you take Henry to be your lawful wedded husband?' she repeated.

'No,' said Clarity firmly.

Everyone gasped.

Tansy's heart missed a beat and then soared. Henry's mouth dropped open. Cleo dropped her wand.

'Pardon?'

The registrar was clearly at a loss for words.

'I said no!' Clarity's voice rang out over the castle ruins. 'Why would I want to do a thing like that?'

'CLARITY!' Henry's face was puce and he was scratching his underarms furiously. He looked as if he was about to burst a blood vessel. 'Darling!'

'Don't you "darling" me, ' she spat, turning to face the congregation. 'I'm not marrying Henry Fazackerley because he is a liar and a cheat, a fraud and a womanizer. Kyle, would you come here?'

Everyone turned as from behind the stonework of the ramparts, Kyle stepped forward, his jaw working with emotion.

'What the blazes ...?' Henry turned pale and clutched at Clarity's arm. She shook him off.

'This is Kyle, everyone,' said Clarity. 'You remember Kyle, Henry? The son of the woman you cheated?'

Henry's eyes were bulging from their sockets.

'Henry promised to marry Kyle's mum,' Clarity announced, her voice shaking a little. 'And then he stole her life savings and did a runner.'

Cries of 'No!' and 'Shame!' echoed from the assembled crowd.

'You don't do that to people, Henry.'

Henry edged away, but Clarity took his arm firmly.

'And,' she went on, 'you're not doing that to me. I am not marrying you, not today, not ...'

And then it was all too much.

Clarity's voice cracked, and tears began to trickle down her face.

A babble of conversation broke out as everyone rushed up to Clarity.

'Darling, how frightful for you!' Diana Greenway enveloped her in a hug. 'And after I'd found you that lovely dress.'

'Clarity, I'm so very sorry,' murmured Angela Vine. 'You were so brave. And you can do better than Henry.'

'Mum, you did the right thing!' Tansy put her arm round her. 'Honestly you did!'

'It's good to see you've grown up at last,' began her grandmother.

'Gran?' Tansy said

'Yes?'

'Shut up!'

'Right,' said her grandmother.

1.05 p.m.

Reflections

'How odd,' whispered Cleo's mother to Angela Vine, 'that Val seemed to recognize Henry. You don't think ...'

'After today,' muttered Angela, 'I really don't know what to think.'

1.10 p.m.

In hot pursuit

'Oh no, you don't!' Kyle grabbed Henry's arm as he strode off down the hill. 'You owe my mother money and I intend to get it.'

'I stole nothing!' spat Henry. 'The money was in a joint account so in the eyes of the law it was as much mine as hers.'

'You are despicable!' shouted Kyle. 'At least give her half of it back.'

'Can't,' smirked Henry. 'It's all gone.'

'So that's why you wanted to latch on to someone else, is it?' yelled Kyle. 'Well, I intend to see you never do this to anyone ever again! Get it?'

Henry was too busy scratching to reply.

1.15 p.m.

'Where's Kyle?' Holly asked Tansy as they hovered around wondering what to do next.

Tansy gestured into the distance.

'Henry did a bunk and Kyle went after him,' she said. 'I have a feeling there is quite a bit he needs to say.'

'Do you know where he lives?' asked Holly.

Tansy shook her head.

'Oh.' Holly looked crestfallen.

'We do have his phone number though,' grinned Tansy.

'Oh goody,' said Holly. 'Can I have it?'

'Why?' asked Tansy innocently.

'Use your imagination,' replied Holly.

1.18 p.m.

'Clarity – darling – I ...'

Tansy's grandmother took her daughter's arm.

'I can't pretend that I'm not happy,' she said. 'I mean, I want you to be happy but I felt so sure that Henry –'

'I've been a fool,' wept Clarity.

'No,' her mother assured her gently. 'You've just been human.'

Clarity gave her a thankful smile.

'By the way,' her mother went on, 'what on earth was wrong with Henry? All that scratching and jumping around?'

'Itching powder,' said Clarity. 'I got Diana to sprinkle it on his costume before she delivered it to the hotel. Call me adolescent, but it gave me huge satisfaction.'

'That's my girl!' laughed her mother. 'Never let the wretches get you down.'

1.20 p.m

'A message! Tansy, I've got a message!' Cleo grabbed Tansy's arm and hopped up and down. 'Look!'

Tansy grinned.

'See, I told you – it's bound to be Trig! I've got to go and sort Mum out – you read it and swoon in private!'

1.25 p.m.

'Right, everyone!' Angela Vine held up a hand. 'Clarity wants you all to come back to her house – the party goes on!'

Everyone hesitated, looking at Clarity for confirmation.

'Of course it does,' she said bravely. 'After all, we do

have one thing to celebrate – or rather two! The twins! Let's go!'

1.35 p.m.

Cleo stood rooted to the spot, staring at the phone.

Hi, Cleo! I guess there's something you should know. It was so cool being with you in the UK but now I've met this great girl back home and I think you and I should finish it. I'll always be your friend, but it's time to move on. Hope you understand.
Love, Trig.

She would have re-read the message but she couldn't see through her tears.

1.45 p.m.

'Scott,' said Jade, taking a sip of fruit punch. 'You have to go to America and stay with Trig at Christmas.'

That's a start, she thought.

'But,' Scott gasped, looking alarmed, 'that would mean we were apart.'

'I know,' nodded Jade, taking a deep breath. 'But we can't live in one another's pockets, Scott. I mean, it's been great and I'm really fond of you but ...'

Scott dropped his sausage roll on the floor and stared at her.

'But what?'

'I think we should cool it,' she gabbled. 'It's all getting too intense and I –'

'You don't love me, that's what you're saying, isn't it?' Scott growled.

'No, no ...' She paused. 'Yes. Yes, I guess that's what I'm saying,' she sighed. 'I'm very fond of you, and I'd love you to be my friend but –'

'You can't do this to me!' Scott pleaded. 'I love you. I need you. Please don't do this.'

His eyes were full of tears. Jade took a deep breath and said what she knew she had to say.

'I have to do it, Scott, for my own sake. I'm sorry. There's no other way.'

2.00 p.m.

'I've rung the hospital and they say the babies are fine,' said Angela, pouring Clarity another drink. 'They are tiny and on ventilators but everything looks very good. Oh, and apparently, there's a message for you from Val.'

'Really? What?' asked Clarity.

'She says that she's really sorry about spoiling things ...'

'I hope you told her she hadn't done any such thing!' Angela grinned.

'She was highly relieved to hear that you didn't go through with it,' she said. 'Apparently, she recognized Henry. Kyle's mother was her best friend from school. The shock of realizing that your future husband was the con man that robbed her mate must have sent her into labour.'

Clarity shook her head.

'She had twinges the other day,' she recalled.

'Oh – and there's something else,' frowned Angela. 'She said to tell you, it's not Basil, it's Ginger. Does that make any sense to you?'

Clarity grinned.

'Perfect sense,' she said.

'Oh good,' said Angela.

2.15 p.m.

'He dumped me!' Cleo touched Tansy's shoulder.

'More fool him!' retorted Tansy resolutely. 'Men are idiots.' She glanced at Cleo.

'Are you OK?'

Cleo took a long, deep breath.

'Yes, I'm fine,' she said. 'Actually, I'm glad – I knew deep down, but I kept hoping. It's easier knowing the truth.'

'Good on you!' grinned Tansy. 'Have a vol-au-vent.'

2.30 p.m.

'You are still coming to stay, aren't you?' Holly asked Tansy.

'I've got this so cool idea about –'

'I can't,' sighed Tansy. 'I can't leave Mum, not after all that's happened. Not tonight, anyway. But I'll call you tomorrow.'

'Promise? I need your help. I've got plans.'

'For Kyle?'

'How did you guess?'

'I know you, Holly. It didn't take brains.'

2.40 p.m.

Recriminations

'He just stormed off!' sobbed Jade piteously. 'And now I feel awful – I mean, what if he does something stupid?'

'He won't,' Holly assured her. 'You did the right thing. You can't pretend to love someone if you don't.'

She sighed deeply.

'And you can't pretend not to, when you do,' she added.

6.30 p.m.

Back at Plough Cottages

'It was bound to happen,' declared Tansy's grandmother as Clarity lay up in her bedroom sobbing her heart out. 'She couldn't keep up that front for ever. Poor lamb.'

Tansy sighed.

'You know,' she said, 'you get nicer with age.'

Her grandmother tutted.

'So do you, dear,' she said sweetly.

SUNDAY

6.45 a.m.

Clearing out

'Aaaah!!' Tansy woke with a start. 'What on earth ...?'

The house was reverberating to the sound of thuds and crashes. She jumped out of bed, and rushed on to the landing.

Her mother was standing in her pyjamas hurling things down the stairs.

'MUM! What's going on?'

'I'm just getting rid of every last trace of Henry Fazackerley,' she cried.

She grabbed a briefcase and flung it over the banister.

'Good riddance –' she grabbed a pile of books and hurled those the same way – 'to bad rubbish!'

And then, suddenly, she burst into tears.

'I just can't bear to think about being alone for the rest of my life,' she sobbed.

'You're not alone, Mum, you've got me!' cried Tansy.

'I know, darling,' smiled her mum. 'And I love you to bits. But you'll grow up and leave home, and then ...'

Her voice faltered.

'I'll come back with loads of children and you can babysit them while I get famous,' finished Tansy.

'Tansy, you're impossible!' her mother smiled through her tears.

'Me? Why? What did I say?'

8.30 a.m.

Aiding and abetting

'Tansy? It's Holly. Sorry to ring so early, but I need that phone number. Now.'

'Why?'

'Why? Why do you think? Kyle is fit, really mature and –'

'Probably not available.'

'Tansy Meadows, do you have to spoil everything?' demanded Holly.

'Sorry,' said Tansy. 'Let's just say I've learned the hard way. Here's the number – but don't say I didn't warn you.'

10.30 a.m.

'I love you, Roy,' said Diana, sidling up to him in the kitchen and putting her arms round him.

Roy eyed her suspiciously.

'Have you been overspending again?'

Diana shook her head.

'So what's with the hugs and kisses then?' he asked, kissing her nose.

'I've just realized that all the posh frocks and designer shoes in the world don't matter,' confessed Diana. 'I mean, you can be the grouchiest old muggins in the universe, but you would never cheat on me. Never.'

Roy put his arms round her.

'And I'm not going to overspend ever again,' added Diana. 'I owe it to you.'

'Diana Greenway, I love you,' murmured Roy. 'I really do.'

11.30 a.m.

Seeking help

'Tansy? Holly. Listen, when are you coming over?'

'Later,' promise Tansy. 'As soon as I know Mum's OK.'

'Only I need to know what to say. To Kyle. I mean I have to have an excuse to phone.'

'Why? It's never stopped you in the past.'

'Be serious,' muttered Holly.

'I am,' said Tansy.

2.00 p.m.

Going in for the kill

'Could I speak to Scott Hamill, please? Allegra Webb. It's about homework.'

She waited, fingers crossed behind her back.

'Scott? Allegra. Look, I know this is an awful cheek, but everyone says you're a whizz at French and I'm in the most awful mess with mine – it's detention if I get another C-minus. And I just wondered, could I possibly nip round to your place and ... Jade? No, she didn't say a thing ... Dropped you? Really? I had no idea. You poor thing. Shall I bring doughnuts?'

She crossed two more fingers.

'Great! See you at four o'clock. And Scott? Jade's very immature for her age – she doesn't understand a guy's needs. See you!'

4.00 p.m.

'I shall have to get back home tomorrow,' said Tansy's grandmother to Clarity, who had emerged red-eyed from the bedroom with five bin bags full of Henry's clothes. 'Beth flies in from America on Tuesday and I promised to put her up for a few nights.'

She eyed her daughter anxiously.

'Will you be all right?' she asked.

'Of course,' said Clarity, dumping the bags by the back door.

'And, Mum – is it still OK for me to go to Holly's?' begged Tansy. 'She's got things planned and –'

'I suppose,' sighed Clarity, 'if that's what you really want to do.'

'Well, I won't if you don't want me to ...'

'Actually,' admitted her mum, 'I'd like a few days on my own, to get things straight in my head. Mum's offered to treat me to three days at a health farm, just chilling out. But I don't want you to feel that I'm dumping you on Holly and –'

'I don't!' Tansy asssured her. 'Only ...'

'What?'

'You won't do anything silly, will you? Get involved with someone else in the aerobics class?'

'Oh darling – now would I?'

'Quite probably,' sighed Tansy. And gave her mum a hug.

6 p.m.

The way forward

'I've just had the most awful thought!' gasped Clarity.

'What?' Tansy mumbled between mouthfuls of leftovers.

'My ring! Or rather Kyle's mother's ring – I should have given it to him to take back to her.'

'Perhaps she doesn't want reminding of Henry,' suggested Tansy.

'That's not the point, ' said Clarity. 'It's legally hers. She can sell it or something. But I haven't a clue how to get in touch with Kyle.'

'I have,' grinned Tansy. 'And I know someone who would be only too pleased to help.'

7 p.m.

'So there's your excuse!' cried Tansy down the phone. 'Ring Kyle and tell him about the ring, and then when he says he'll come and collect it, you can sort of appear at the crucial moment.'

'Brilliant!' cried Holly. 'That is so cool. I'll call you right back.'

7.30 p.m.

'He's coming up on Tuesday after work,' Holly told Tansy. 'Only, would you mind awfully if you kind of weren't hanging around, because he might just fancy you and not me and that would scupper all my plans and –'

'No problem,' agreed Tansy. 'I'll be seeing Andy and cooing over babies!'

'Oh goody,' murmured Holly.

'Just one thing,' asked Tansy.

'What?'

'Paul,' teased Tansy. 'You remember, the guy you would love for ever? What about him?'

'There are times,' said Holly, 'when mature women have to move on. And this is one of them. Now, what do you think I should wear?'